Dark Companion

Also by Jim Nisbet

Novels

The Gourmet (1981) (reprinted as The Damned
Don't Die; 1986)

Lethal Injection (1987)

Death Puppet (1989)

Ulysses' Dog (published in French only; 1993)

Prelude to a Scream (1997)

The Price of the Ticket (2003)

The Syracuse Codex (2005)

How I Got Work; or, What Junk Can Do for You!
  (forthcoming, 2007)

Poetry

Poems for a Lady (1979)

Gnachos for Bishop Berkeley (1980)

Morpho (with Alastair Johnston; 1982)

Small Apt (with photos by Shelly Vogel; 1982)

Across the Tasman Sea (1997)

Nonfiction

Laminating the Conic Frustrum (1991)

Recordings

The Visitor (1984)

Dark Companion

Jim Nisbet

FIRST EDITION
Published April 2006
(A French edition appeared in 2005)

Dustjacket and interior artwork
by Carol Collier.

ISBN 0-939767-54-6

Dennis McMillan Publications
4460 N. Hacienda del Sol (Guest House)
Tucson, Arizona 85718
Tel. (520)-529-6636 email: dennismcmillan@aol.com
website: http://dennismcmillan.com

ACKNOWLEDGMENTS

One really can't say enough or learn enough about the physics of compact objects, nor of the minds that are and have been fascinated by the subject. But the author is specifically indebted to several texts, prime among them Simon Mitton's elegant and eminently readable *The Crab Nebula,* as well as *The Supernova Story* by Laurence A. Marschall. Hardcore readers who may spend a couple of hours with the present tale will find a couple of years' worth of contemplation within the covers of *Black Holes, White Dwarfs, and Neutron Stars* by Stuart L. Shapiro and Saul A. Teukolsky. In between reside a number of classic, demanding, and readable texts, including Stephen W. Hawking's *A Brief History of Time; The Meaning of Relativity* by Albert Einstein; Janna Levin's *How The Universe Got Its Spots;* Kip S. Thorne's *Black Holes and Time Warps; New Frontiers in Astronomy* in the READINGS FROM SCIENTIFIC AMERICAN series— particularly the monographs "The Nature of Pulsars" by Jeremiah P. Ostriker and "The Search for Black Holes" by Kip S. Thorne; *One Day Celestial Navigation* by Otis S. Brown, and, what the hell, *Sailing Alone Around the World* by Captain Joshua S. Slocum.

Last but not least, a double-barreled thanks to Peelhead and Captain Josh Prior for a story about a slippery pistol.

Dark Companion

Holding a grudge is like letting somebody
live rent-free in your head.

—Roadside sign, Ogden, N.C.

"There is too much freedom in this country."

—Mohamed Atta

ONE

Banerjhee Rolf was sprinkling chlorinated glacial runoff on his zinnias when Toby Pride draped his arms over their mutual fence.

"Man," Pride suggested lazily, "if mushrooms grew here, we could call this place Paradise."

Banerjhee sublimated his wince into an uncomprehending frown. "Why mushrooms, my gainfully unemployed friend?"

Pride, whose unshaven mien and disheveled hair reinforced his aura of lassitude, merely stared. After a moment, Banerjhee realized that Pride was watching the little rainbows evoked by sunlight from the umbrella of spray that billowed from the hose nozzle. He adjusted his track over the yard so that it would soon be watering the Baby's Tears and various ferns happily populating the shadows beneath the lone redwood that towered over the back fence. No sunlight, no rainbows, and, thus, no momentary delight to be shared with his seedy neighbor.

Pride seemed not to notice. He turned his left wrist upside down to display a clutch of lottery tickets. "Today's the day, BJ, my ungainfully unemployed friend. And I am here to help you."

1

Banerjhee arced the descent of his hose away from the shade so that he faced the Krauss fence, opposite Pride's. The Krauss family was gone nine or ten months a year in their land yacht, and he liked that about them. Pride, on the other hand, rented his place from an owner Banerjhee had never met.

"She's up to eighty-two million smackers." Pride snapped a fingernail against the slips. "You need to get in on it."

Banerjhee's idea of winning the lottery was different from Toby Pride's. So far as Banerjhee was concerned, a man had a better chance of shutting two one-dollar bills in a box in a damp corner with the hope that they would mate than he had of winning a jackpot in which millions of people guess at a set of six two-digit numbers. The chance of correctly guessing that sequence is precisely one in ten to the twelfth power, or one in a trillion. That is a very low probability. Anyway, never mind, for who listened to Banerjhee Rolf? Was there any doubt that every last smiley-face magnet in California pinned at least one lottery ticket to a refrigerator door?

As Banerjhee knew, Pride had his own gaming philosophy, and it was simple. Every week Pride purchased two lottery tickets. If the jackpot went over ten million, he bought two more; twenty million, another two; thirty million, two more for a total of six, and so forth.

The irony, as Banerjhee supposed, was that in a sense Toby Pride had already won a lottery. The guy didn't work; he had visitors at all hours and plenty of money. His pretty girlfriend liked to take her sun in their backyard practically naked. There were no kids to be seen or heard, and, his house having been run down by a long series of community college students, Pride's rent was cheap. Though he was equivocal beyond modesty about the source of his income, Pride had once offered to Banerjhee that he was an only child whose folks lived on the East Coast and despised him sufficiently to pay him an annuity with the stipulation that he neither contact them nor venture more easterly than Salt Lake City. Not least because Pride considered it a bargain, the arrangement amused him. He'd been a little drunk at the time of this revelation, and hadn't mentioned it since.

Insofar as Banerjhee knew Toby Pride at all, he sympathized with the parents. What might any parent have done in a previous incarnation to deserve such a child? Pride stayed mildly inebriated all his waking hours, yet drove his car whenever he felt like it. A very discreet car it was, too, a top-of-the-line BMW, entirely black with tinted windows, whose anonymity was only slightly betrayed by cookie-cutter alloy wheels and fat, low-profile tires. A closer look revealed that those wheels were backed up by huge brake calipers, which subtended an extremely slippery roof line whose silhouette rendered its back seat almost useless. Throw in a split exhaust, a five-speed automatic transmission, a cam that revved its V8 up to 7600 rpm with the near-instant acceleration of a fastballed ninja star. . . . Pride had told him all about it. It was an expensive street machine, designed to go fast in safety, with a base price well over $70,000. When Pride offered to take him for a ride, Banerjhee turned him down.

From the shade of his redwood Banerjhee appraised his east fence, or, more specifically, the bamboo shoots he had planted along the foot of it. The in-house horticulturist at a local gardening center had told him that this bamboo, fertilized and watered, would form a nearly impenetrable barrier of thickly knuckled stalks with sharp-edged, sword-like leaves just as high as he pleased within eighteen months of planting the starts.

Fourteen months to go.

He squinted toward the sun, which was just touching the gable of the Krauss home. No question of whether bamboo or anything else would be receiving enough insolation in

3

California. Maybe the tender shoots were scorched? Not likely. No doubt some would survive, some would not. Some would get tall, some would remain stunted. He'd seen a wall of bamboo forty feet high in a graveled planter box alongside a skyscraper in downtown San Francisco. That wall faced west. So did his side of Pride's fence; he watered it every day.

The horticulturist mentioned that the giant panda of China favored this species of bamboo for the nourishment afforded by its highest and most tender leaves. By coincidence, stuffed toy pandas, too big to fit into the back seat of Pride's BMW, were currently being given away by a petroleum multinational via local gas stations as part of a campaign to promote the corporate sensitivity to global ecology. Perhaps Banerjhee would patronize this chain and lay in a supply of stuffed pandas against the day when his bamboo would be tall and sturdy enough to support them, which would also initiate the anniversary of the renewed privacy of his backyard.

Until then, he and Toby Pride would have to get along.

"I bought extras for you, BJ." Pride fanned the slips of paper. "Gimme two bucks and take your pick."

Still in the shade of his redwood and watering the head-high impatiens refulgent in the corner formed by the back fence and the Krauss fence, his back to Pride, Banerjhee narrowed his eyes. "I don't gamble, Toby. As I've told you many times."

"This ain't gambling, BJ." Pride hooked his armpits over the fence and leaned on it until it creaked, his arms extended over the bamboo shoots. He shuffled the tickets and fanned them. "This is like taking chalk from the cliffs of Dover." Banerjhee turned from the umbrella of water to look at him, and Pride chuckled. "One day one of them is certain to make its mark."

Banerjhee frowned. It happened that he had been to Dover. He knew the cliffs were chalk, had wandered among the ancient hand-hewn tunnels to be found in them, and had gazed toward the cloud bank that hovered over the west coast of Nord-Pas-de-Calais, not twenty-five miles across the Dover Strait.

To discover that a fellow American knew anything at all of the greater world always surprised Banerjhee, but he suspected that the cliffs of Dover must have been mentioned in a recent documentary on one of the travel channels, so favored by the consumerate as to have nearly displaced in it any urge to explore the world from some vantage other than a reclining chair.

Pride had neatly synthesized this hermeticism in a discussion of the events of September 11, 2001. Emerging from an all-day marathon of televised reprise of the airliner attacks on New York to find Banerjhee weeding among the Baby's Tears, Pride stood at the fence for a long time. Finally, Banerjhee had asked him if he were okay.

"BJ," Pride said, confusion brightening his eyes, "what did America ever do to deserve it?"

"Everything," Banerjhee had assured him; for surely, any other answer would not do. "For example," he told Pride, "America embraced my parents when they got off the boat in Vancouver, Washington, in 1945, and gave them a chance that few other nations could or would. Just like," he suggested, "it must have done for your own progenitors, too, whenever they got here?"

Pride only blinked and said, "They hate us."

Banerjhee wondered whether Pride knew anything at all about his progenitors.

"Two bucks, BJ," Pride insisted, "equals a shot at 82 million smackers. And don't forget, you could win some dipshit other amount, too. A hundred thou say. Or fifty bucks. You always win something eventually. One of my pet lottery theories is that the longer you don't win anything, the more likely it is that Fate or Destiny or Mojo–whatever–is setting you up for the big enchilada."

Banerjhee did not suppress a monosyllabic grunt.

Pride cast a glance around the yard without looking directly at Banerjhee's garage, beyond which the Econoline van, having sucked a valve in its own driveway three months before, waited on sagging tires for Banerjhee to get serious about fixing it. They still had the old blue Peugeot in which Madja carpooled to work one day a week; otherwise it was at his disposal, so. . . .

"Yes, Toby," Banerjhee said almost cheerfully. "A hundred thousand dollars would be most appreciated. But, you know. . . ."

"Yes? What?"

"Money can't buy happiness."

Toby Pride shook his head. "Oh, fuck it, BJ, are you such a glass half-full kinda guy you couldn't use a little supplementary income?"

Truthfully Banerjhee had to wonder at the answer to that question. Because he did not fly an American flag off his front porch, certain of his suburban neighbors shunned him and made no bones about the reason. Not that being embraced by these same people would make his life complete, but it might make it a little more . . . frictionless. What did money have to do with that?

"Happiness," Banerjhee said aloud, "is a low coefficient of friction."

"Money," Pride responded without missing a beat, "is the next best thing to a waterbed and a bottle of olive oil."

Banerjhee didn't want to chuckle, but he did. Pride, it seemed, had a notion of friction.

"And," Pride nodded, as if being very deliberate about dispensing his wisdom, "it don't stink so bad."

Banerjhee had long since realized that Toby Pride was

nowhere nearly so stupid as he generally acted. Were Banerjhee to be asked, in fact, he would declare Pride possessed of a distinct cunning; animal cunning, as some people called it. A further assessment struck him as more accurate: Toby Pride was ever rapacious for a buck and far from punctilious about how he went about getting it. Taking money from his parents to stay clear of them was, in Toby's book, a no-brainer.

As for the rest? Televised sports, canned beer, and seedless marijuana just about summed it up. So far as Banerjhee was concerned, Toby Pride lived about as doltish an existence as one could imagine. The facts were hard to construe another way. Pride's own back yard provided his own metaphor. This contained a leaky hot tub of the redwood cask type, surrounded by a certain amount of brown grass, perhaps knee high, choked by leaves descended from a bay laurel and a lemon tree, the latter nearly deceased despite the odd *sub rosa* spritz from over the fence. Against Pride's back fence stood a rambling barbecue pit. Crafted of river rock by a previous owner and large enough to bake bread and grill meat and so forth, it had fallen into such desuetude that grass was growing out of the rain-saturated lumps of its last charcoal fire, long forgotten, and finches nested in one of its two chimneys. Banerjhee liked the finches. Madja had taken to feeding them, and so the good comes with the bad. Half-way across Pride's yard a bottle of suntan lotion lay atop Pride's girlfriend's nylon-webbed chaise lounge, which was parked in the wake of a rusted power mower. The grass exited the back of the mower about shin high, but in front retained its knee-high stature. And there you had it—or, at least, there Banerjhee had it, his metaphor; Toby Pride's mind had progressed just so far on its path through life, far enough to learn how to feed and care for its vessel. Having achieved this modest summit, there it had stalled. And yet Toby Pride was as happy as a dog lying on his side in a ray of sunshine on a hand-knotted rug. Most curious.

"BJ," Pride insisted, using a tone indicative of great seriousness of intent. "Take the tickets. It's two bucks." Pride looked down on Banerjhee's side of the fence. "These damn bamboo sets cost more than that, each."

Indeed they had. Although Banerjhee resented being manipulated, and he loathed squandering any money at all, he wearily capitulated with the hope that if he spent the two dollars, maybe Pride would leave him to his more or less frictionless backyard chores, at peace for the time being.

"Give me that pen," Pride said.

Banerjhee glanced at his own shirt front. Of course he had a mechanical pencil in his pocket. He handed it to Pride.

Pride closed his eyes and shuffled his lottery tickets. He opened his eyes and drew a line across two tickets, snapping the lead on the second one. "What the fuck is this?" He squinted at the pencil tip, figured it out, and adjusted it. "Delicate little fucker. Here." He folded the unmarked tickets into his own shirt pocket. "These are your tickets." He showed the two marked ones. "If you don't buy them and one of them wins, I'm going to bring it out here and taunt you with it before I cash it in. BJ, I'm going to say, but for your unbelievable cheapness and lack of faith in the basic order underlying the randomness of events, here went your good fortune. I am going to take this ticket down to the liquor store, cash it in, and buy me a nice. . . ." Pride's face clouded over. "A nice. . . ."

"College education," Banerjhee suggested, taking tickets and pencil. Each ticket was a thin slip of coated white stock not unlike thermal fax paper, with black numbers and a barcode superimposed on an orange logo. Super Lotto Plus. He'd never held one before.

Pride rolled his eyes. "BJ, listen to me," he said sternly. "If you was to win eighty-two million dollars—it'll be more by Wednesday—what in the fuck would you want a college education for? Huh? What for? So you could spend the next twenty years working up to forty grand a year in some asshole factory?" Pride laughed. "Making assholes?" He screwed up his eyes and appeared to study the upper branches of Banerjhee's redwood. "Earning roughly one twenty-first of the jackpot in your entire career and get the heart attack anyway? Is that your deal with fatalism or something, my friend?"

I'm not a fatalist, Banerjhee telepathed as he pulled out his billfold, and I'm not your friend. He handed Toby a pair of singles, wryly noting that the gesture orphaned a twenty. "Go in peace and good fortune," he said mildly. "But especially peace."

Pride showed a broad grin and accepted the two dollars. "Exactly what I was going to say. Good luck. Touch your rabbit foot. Kiss the blarney stone. No whistling. Peace on you. Do you know that if you get enough channels, you can watch reruns of *Star Trek* interfucked by live bicycle races from Europe all day long?"

Banerjhee watched the barefoot Toby Pride wade back through the grass to his flagstone patio. Much faded by the sun, a dinged and oft-patched surfboard leaned against the patio overhang. Banerjhee wondered if Pride ever used the board. So far as he remembered, it had leaned thus for six months. The Pacific Ocean was sixty miles away. There was no surfboard rack atop Pride's sleek BMW. Pride probably kept a guitar he never played, too. Maybe he kept the stuffed effigy of a man as well, the man he might have been, the man he never had been or would be, the man that was, after all, some other than the one he had become.

Diversity, Banerjhee thought, as he went back to watering his yard, is what makes America great. Once more he fell to

9

contemplating the idea of a bamboo fence behind him. In front of him, the pinkish-mauve blossoms of the impatiens wavered in a passing breeze; so named because its ripe pods burst open at a touch.

TWO

*There was a wattled fence over which some ivy-like
creeper spread its cool green leaves, and among the
leaves were white flowers with petals half-unfolded
like the lips of people smiling at their own thoughts.*

Meditating as he watered the impatiens, Banerjhee almost
always came around to recalling this passage from the
Tale of Genji. It made him smile, too. Like a man with his
own thoughts.

The impatiens didn't really look that way—they weren't
white and they weren't shy—but their percussive pods
resembled a smiling face; sort of; sort of the opposite of a
eucalyptus button, whose face is hidden as if in accordance
with the etymology of its name, which means 'hidden' or
'concealed'. Interesting. . . .

"BJ, wait."

Banerjhee's smile faded. "Yes, Toby?" He turned to face his
neighbor.

Pride stood on his side of the fence, much as before, but he
wasn't alone. Alongside him, draped over him more or less,
stood a woman with dark blonde hair. The sun had slowly
kissed what skin was visible around her halter top to a
luminescent tan, underwritten by a flawless complexion that

probably glowed as if it were facing a California sunset every hour of the day. Her eyes were a startling emerald color, and clearly she was very stoned. This did not stop her from smiling, however, as Toby introduced her.

"Esme, BJ. BJ, Esme."

Well, well. Introduced after six months. Come to reconnoiter, Banerjhee squinted, it was a brassiere. Diaphanous, lacy, and mauve.

"Charmed, Miss." Banerjhee averted his eyes and bowed slightly, and the hose lightly misted the tops of his shoes.

"I was thinking, BJ." Toby passed the flat of his hand over Esme's shoulders. "One of them flowers over there would look real good in Esme's hair. Yes? No?"

Esme, to give her a little credit, blushed. But her mind was on the impatiens, too.

"I was thinking it would go real nice with her hair, her eyes, her skin and, uh–" Toby inserted a finger beneath the back strap of Esme's undergarment and ran it from shoulder blade to shoulder blade, "–her clothes."

"Such as they are," Banerjhee smiled. He'd been wondering why Pride was getting around to introducing Esme, and now he knew. Pride wanted something.

Esme straightened up, squared her shoulders, and emitted a blinding smile.

"Oh," Toby assured him, "they are such."

Banerjhee crossed the yard to pluck an impatiens blossom, and walked it back to the fence. "Here we are."

Rather than take it from him, Esme inclined her head slightly. Toby nodded approvingly and, after some hesitation, Banerjhee secured the flower in the girl's hair, using a tiny mauve clip he found there, just above her right temple. The hair was soft, the skin even softer and warm, and about her hung a pleasant odor of tanning oil.

"Man," Toby said to Esme, "that flower is perfect."

"You think so?" Esme said shyly, rolling her eyes toward the flower, which she could not see, and gingerly touching it with her fingertips.

"If I thought our relationship was gonna last past next week," Toby said, "I would put in a standing order for them."

"Oh," said the girl coolly, "let's not rush."

"Not any more than we already have," Toby laughed.

Esme giggled.

"Drawing's tomorrow, BJ," Toby said, taking Esme's hand. "Don't forget it."

Banerjhee frowned.

"The lottery," Toby reminded him. "You got a ticket. Two tickets. Where are they?"

Banerjhee recollected himself and reached for his shirt pocket, where he found only the mechanical pencil. He went to one hip pocket, then the other. There they were. He produced them and smiled feebly.

Toby shook his head. "Says right on the back not to iron those suckers." He held out his hand. "Maybe I should keep them for you after all?"

Banerjhee offered the tickets. Toby shook his head. "BJ, I got to tell you. If you give me that ticket and that sucker hits, I'm going to cash it in and hand you one of my other tickets and tell you you got skunked and you won't even know the difference." Toby showed smoke-yellowed teeth in a false smile. "Right?"

As if to prompt Banerjhee, Esme nodded.

"Right." Banerjhee put the tickets into his shirt pocket.

"Right," Toby repeated. "The stupidvision says it's up to 89 million. We're off to buy two more tickets. It'll be over ninety by the time we get to the store. Esme says business first, fun later. She's got a head for business." He glanced approvingly at Esme, who smiled shyly. "And fun," Toby added. He looked back at Banerjhee. "Get two more for you, too?

Buck a throw? Maybe you got a personal number you want to try?" Toby narrowed his eyes. "Didn't your people invent astrology?"

Esme brightened. "My best girlfriend's mom played some numbers relating somehow to her trine and when she ran out, she threw in two pairs of numbers from her cellphone bill and won one hundred dollars."

Toby whistled and inclined his head. "One hundred dollars."

Esme nodded eagerly. "She bought pizza and beer and fed the whole block."

Pizza, Banerjhee thought to himself, isn't really food.

"And then I bet," Toby prompted sagely, "she bought two more lottery tickets."

"So she actually won ninety-eight dollars," Banerjhee pointed out, "minus the price of however many tickets she'd bought in the first place."

"Cost of doing business," Esme confirmed. "She's like you, Toby. She buys tickets every week."

"Have you ever won, Toby?" Banerjhee asked.

Pride nodded. "Twice. Never more than a thousand bucks, though."

"Pretty good. In how many years of play?"

Toby shrugged. "Since they started the fucking thing."

"And you buy tickets every week?"

"Depends on the jackpot."

"But sure he does," Esme put in.

"Sure I do," Toby agreed, annoyed, as if the information were too specific or too personal.

"And you, Miss Esme?"

"I always mean to but, most weeks, I don't get around to it," Esme offered, adding apologetically, "Most organic markets don't sell Lotto tickets."

"That's not true, baby," Toby interjected. "There's one in Oakland that sells tickets."

"Right," Esme said, "Oakland. Like I'm there *at all.*"

"A girl can dream."

"Ugh. I hate Oakland."

Toby shrugged. "You should go over there more often. Join a health club or something. Get used to hanging out with people who have money."

"Yeah?" Esme said, suddenly showing a worldliness that Banerjhee, for one, had not suspected. "When's that going to start?"

Toby pursed his lips. "Just as soon as they announce them numbers on Wednesday. Tomorrow." He passed his hand around her waist and whispered theatrically, "Stick around, baby."

"Gross." Esme squirmed away.

Toby just laughed.

Banerjhee couldn't help but notice that the side seams of Esme's denim cutoffs were slit all the way up to the belt loops, and that she wore a diaphanous mauve thong beneath them.

"C'mere you little rabbit," Toby said.

"No!" Esme squealed. "Sex fiend. Help."

Toby chased Esme through the patio door and into the house, wherein something fell to the floor, a lamp or an ashtray or a book—check that—maybe the TV remote. Laughter ensued.

Banerjhee noticed that his hose had completely soaked his shoes.

Barefoot inside his own house he ran into his wife, Madja, just returning home from her job. She kissed him on the cheek and said, "Email from Sam today."

"Oh?"

"The department has offered a teaching position for the summer."

"Paid?"

"Of course. But he's going to have to struggle until then."

15

"Naturally. It's good for a student to struggle. But perhaps he'll never have to struggle like you did."

She hung her jacket in the hall closet and patted his cheek. "He'll never have to struggle like we did. You've seen to that."

Banerjhee wasn't so sure about that, but he accepted the compliment. "So now, with three years to go, he'll be in Chicago full time."

"That's true. If we want to see him, we'll have to go there ourselves."

Banerjhee pursed his lips. "Expensive."

Madja bustled into the kitchen, rolling her sleeves as she went. "We've been charging all of our groceries to that airline credit card. A lot of miles have accrued."

"Enough for the two of us?"

She rinsed her hands at the sink, shaking her head. "One?"

Madja studied the back yard through the window beyond the sink. "We have miles sufficient for a single round trip."

Banerjhee considered this. "It took one year of buying groceries to save enough points for a single plane ticket to Chicago?"

Madja looped the hand towel through the handle on the refrigerator. "Have you eaten?"

"Of course not."

"Lunch?"

He shrugged.

Madja showed concern. "Are you losing your appetite?"

Banerjhee shook his head. "I just forgot."

Madja's frown did not entirely overcome her smile. "Neutron stars?"

Banerjhee smiled too. "Fascinating."

"And weird," she added, before he could say it.

"Both," he agreed. "A physics lab in the heavens." He looked at her suddenly. "How did you know?"

"I don't. You do."

He nodded. "Someday I'll explain them to you."

She patted his cheek. "BJ, I'm an accountant, not a mathematician."

She'd called him BJ for thirty-two years and it griped Banerjhee that, overhearing her use it, Toby Pride had appropriated it. "But you don't need to be a mathematician to–"

Madja was looking into the refrigerator. "But it helps. How about a nice glass of chilled white wine?"

"Will wine help?"

"I think so." She retrieved a bottle of Chardonnay, which they'd opened the night before, from the door shelf and handed it over her shoulder. "What was that?"

Banerjhee cocked his head and listened. "It sounds like Mr. Pride explaining to his girlfriend what he would like her to do for him."

"He has a new one?"

Banerjhee retrieved two stemmed wineglasses from a cabinet on the other side of the sink. "Same one. Her name, I've learned at last, is Esme."

"Maybe that boy's settling down."

"He's not a boy. He's divorced."

"I forgot. Plus he's a dope dealer."

"You don't know that."

"I have eyes, don't I?"

Banerjhee poured each glass half full. "Live and let live, as us hypocrites say, right before we call the Secret Witness Hotline, with the result that he gets replaced by five or six college students."

Loud laughter came over the fence.

"Remember when a tenant over there tried to force us to cut down the redwood because it interfered with his satellite television reception?"

Two car doors slammed.

Banerjhee narrowed his eyes. "Lucidly."

Pride's Beamer fired up and its tires chirped as it backed into the street.

Kneeling before the refrigerator, Madja selected various packages and plastic storage bins and set them on the counter. "Mm, moldy asparagus with penne in gelid olive oil. Whew."

She handed a plastic container over her shoulder. Banerjhee, smiling indulgently, relayed it to the trash can under the sink. "We'll never eat all the leftovers you save. There aren't enough of us."

"When we lived in San Francisco," Madja said into the refrigerator, "there was always a homeless person to give them to."

"Yes," Banerjhee reflected. "Either before we got back to the car from the restaurant or before we got from the car to the apartment."

"Always," she confirmed. "I can't break the habit. I hate to throw away food. Such portions they give you nowadays."

"Especially in Indian restaurants," Banerjhee reminded her.

"It's scandalous," Madja agreed, without much fervor. "Speaking of which, there's a curry in here."

Banerjhee sipped his wine and gazed out the sink window, where the setting sun bathed the top third of the redwood tree in resplendent gold. "No thanks."

Madja raised the lid on a plastic bin, sniffed suspiciously, and raised the lid further. "It is a little dated, I think."

"Darling, we went to that restaurant some two weeks ago. Maybe three." They allowed themselves to eat out once a month.

She frowned. "The one in Concord?"

"The Star."

She handed the container to him and returned to shuffling others in the refrigerator. "We could make a tajeen."

Banerjhee dumped the container's contents into the trash can and closed the cabinet door. "That's two hours. Three if we shop for ingredients."

"True."

"I'll create one on Saturday."

"Okay." Madja thought a moment. "So what about tonight?"

"One of your omelets."

Madja sat back on her heels and watched him rinse the container. When he turned off the water and took up the dish towel, she went back to rummaging. "Eggs."

Banerjhee watched her as he dried the lid. She was dark and slim. A few laugh lines trailed back from the corners of her large, black eyes, but hardly a wrinkle traced the smoothness of her face. Her hair was long and, excepting a dramatic streak of gray at her left temple, it remained as black as the day he'd met her. They had been married for thirty years, and he loved her very much. "But will that be enough for you, BJ?" she asked the refrigerator. "Are you sure?"

"I am sure. A light meal will make for a pleasant two or three hours of reading after dinner."

"Very well. That sounds good to me, too."

"How about you? Did you have lunch?"

She stood with her arms full of an egg carton and a quart of milk, scallions and jack cheese, and closed the refrigerator door with her shoulder. "No. Yes. At the conference table."

"A meeting?"

She set about arranging the ingredients on the counter next to the stove. "No. The new intern didn't show up this morning, leaving almost all of her work unfinished. It came down to me or it wasn't going to get done. Thus," she shrugged, "lunch."

"Not even a snack?"

"Imogene brought me back a coffee and some sushi."

19

"Yuck," Banerjhee said.

Madja shrugged. "It wasn't bad, actually." She took a sip of wine. "This is better." She touched the rim of her glass to his. "This is much better."

THREE

Technically speaking, Banerjhee knew a lot more about mushrooms than Toby Pride ever would. One might say that, if Pride knew mushrooms from the outside in, Banerjhee knew them from the inside out.

Ever since he and Sam and Madja moved from San Francisco to Walnut Creek, Banerjhee had been a pharmacologist for SynBad, Inc. Actually, while his degree was in organic chemistry with a minor in mathematics and graduate work in pharmacology, his company isolated and synthesized compounds from native plant medicines, and Banerjhee ran its quality control lab. He and his assistants sampled and tested output, an important task which Banerjhee took very seriously. His predecessor, seeing a test that revealed a slight anomaly or contamination, would shrug and dismiss it with his favorite homily, "If it's good enough for monkeys, it's good enough for humans." Banerjhee's laboratory, on the other hand, set a standard for the industry.

By and by the four chemists who founded the firm took it public, convened a new board of directors, and began to divest themselves of their interest. All four retired within six months of each other. Three pooled funds and bought a winery in Napa. Within a year the fourth died, of an aneurysm, on a

21

golf course. Without exception, once these men whom Banerjhee had seen nearly every day for some twelve years departed the company, he never heard from them again.

Soon venture capitalists invaded the boardroom, executives were headhunted from the far reaches of a nebulous and international pool of management talent, and corporate money began to flow uphill. Debt increased. Research was radically curtailed. An "Executive Vice President for Human Resources" was contracted to clean house. When the last targeted employee had been fired or forced into early retirement, the HR VP's contract expired. Thus, went board-room reasoning, there would be no one among management on whom remaining personnel might focus resentment. After a visit accompanied by two suits bearing clipboard and palmtop, this executive declared Banerjhee's lab, despite being perhaps the most efficient and vital department in the company, as overstaffed and expensive, noting that much of what it did could be outsourced at two-thirds the cost. Before his eyes, Banerjhee's department was decimated. Talent and resources evaporated. Soon he was running studies and writing up results by himself at night and on weekends to keep up. Madja noticed the strain but said nothing, for she knew he loved his work.

In the meantime, Sam passed through his junior and senior years of high school and had already spent a year at college, more or less while Banerjhee wasn't looking.

Finally the pressure became so great and conditions so intol-erable that Banerjhee accepted a severance—enough to see Sam through two or maybe three thrifty years on partial scholarship at college—in lieu of almost certain burnout. However, Banerjhee found it hard to regard the severance deal other than by the light of failure. He had never quit a job in his life, had never given up on a project, had never let down an employer, had never been fired, but his termination smacked of all four. It reeked of unfairness too but, before he had time to catch his breath, SynBad was sold to a conglomerate that controlled several "baby bell" phone companies, a hubcap and wheel manufacturer, a few radio stations, a cable television market, a national chain of dive shops, a swim suit manufacturer, a 150-year-old Hong-Kong manufacturer of herbal hard-on pills, and a small company that produced five-thousand-dollar carbon-fiber niblicks. The first thing they did was change the locks. The second thing they did was take all of SynBad's employee entitlements and benefits—which included Banerjhee's retirement package and 401-K, the unexercised stock options which made up about half of his severance, and his health insurance—to court, with the legally intriguing argument that, since these liabilities had been incurred under a previous management, the new management had no obligation to meet or fulfill them.

Fourteen years of faithful service.

As representative of a small group of senior employees, Banerjhee met with the new company's new Human Resources vice-president, who, having accepted without a glance a thick folio outlining certain legal, ethical, and health insurance issues, forestalled Banerjhee's explanations with a raised hand.

"Listen, Mr. . . ." she glanced at her appointment calendar, "Mr. Rolf. Let's get something straight." She told off a ringed finger on one hand with the brightly polished nail of its opposite's forefinger. "The present owners of SynBad, Inc., have but one interest, and that is to cut the fat so as to brighten up the bottom line, thereby enabling them to sell the company at a profit while paying off various rather onerous junk bond obligations they incurred in the leveraged buyout. Existing entitlements comprise some forty-eight percent of that fat; it's an obvious target; you can't expect them not to go after it." Various bracelets rattled on her wrists as she moved the telling forefinger. "Two." She looked over the fingers into his eyes. "It's nothing personal."

Escorted by a young security guard to the door, Banerjhee wandered across the parking lot and finally stood, not quite arrived at the Econoline, stock still, as if stunned. He had never experienced it before, but now he sensed beneath the mellow ambiance of the California environment a harsh and ominous undercurrent. The bright sunlight, formerly a matter for blinking happily before donning sunglasses, now became oppressive, almost insidious, perhaps even dangerous, much as it might be perceived by a man in an open dingy on a limitless sea with no propulsion, no shirt, and no water. The cool layer of Pacific air that often reaches so far inland, bringing with it a taste of salt and a hint of the sea, now seemed insufficient to dispel his claustrophobia. The parking lot blistering his feet resolved into its true identity as just another syndrome of a pandemic cancer. It occurred to him that he might become crushed between asphalt and sky. The sight of his ten-year old Econoline, looking as if it had strayed from another pasture into this field of almost militantly new machinery, proffered scant solace. He looked around, as unsteady and uncertain as if he'd just transubstantiated into this unfamiliar video game from some other one whose name he had already forgotten.

A wide and teeming boulevard ran adjacent the parking lot, and across it a magnificent cerise Bougainvillea exploded some three stories up the chimney of a stuccoed villa, as vibrant as a flock of startled redwing blackbirds. Someone had carefully arranged yucca, euphorbia, zinnias, African violets, geraniums, ice plant, various other succulents, and even a fruiting prickly pear cactus around the front and sides of this opulent home, where, carefully tended, all flourished. A Jeep Cherokee stood in the driveway, black and gleaming and so new it still bore a dealer's plate. The home's windows were spotless. The front door stood open. A realtor's A-frame OPEN sign stood on the sidewalk in front of the mailbox.

In a daze, Banerjhee wandered over there. The journey wasn't unconscious. He had to walk parallel to the opposite sidewalk for about an eighth of a mile and press a "Pedestrian" button at a traffic light. After a wait of about ten minutes he scurried across the six lane boulevard, even as the Walk signal conceded to Don't Walk in less than two seconds. As he gained the curb, an idling, ebony Lincoln Navigator, its massive bumper overhanging the crosswalk until the light went green, abruptly accelerated past him, missing the heel of his trailing foot by perhaps eleven inches.

The realtor had a strong Scottish brogue and was very willing to chat up a walk-in. He handed Banerjhee a flyer on which somebody had condensed the many advantages of this home to a single page of text with a picture. Proximity to good schools, restaurants, a health club, shopping, a twelve-screen multiplex, fast food, on-ramps to two freeways and an "excellent corporate neighbor"—perhaps the realtor was fishing for a relocated executive?—with new all-gas kitchen, stainless steel appliances, six-burner restaurant range, maple cabinetry, granite countertops, 3-1/2 marble bath-rooms, three-car garage, three bedrooms, a home theater, upgraded electrical and plumbing, hardwood floors, fireplace, new washer, dryer and roof, wired throughout for fiber optic and cable, one prepaid year remaining on the landscaping contract. . . .

A bargain at $3,495,000.

Banerjhee had a look around, and it appeared to him that, its marquee price notwithstanding, no single feature of the home retained anything of intrinsic or architectural interest. A consultant had furnished a settee, drapes, and fresh flowers for the living area. On the kitchen island stood a bowl of apples, a bottle each of red and white wine in a rack, and two long-stemmed glasses. A poster of John Lennon, hands in pockets and peering at the camera through a pair of granny glasses, hung over the fireplace mantel, bearing the single-word caption, "Imagine. . . ."

Returned to the front door, Banerjhee thought he may as well swap lies with the realtor. "Nice place."

It was mid-afternoon and perhaps there hadn't been many viewers. The realtor looked up from a paperback copy of *Trainspotting* and said, "They don't come any better, my friend, not at this price."

Banerjhee liked the brogue. He glanced at the prospectus. "Three and a half, effectively."

"Place just behind went for almost four not three months ago. There won't be any hold-backs on this baby for a pest inspection, nor roof or foundation either. It's right as rain." He glanced aside and lowered his voice. "There are already four offers near the asking and I've just spoken with a lass who's driving over with her fiancé for a serious look."

"I'm not surprised," Banerjhee assured him. "It's first-rate. And how long has it been on the market?"

"We've only just had the broker's viewing, and this is our first opening to the public."

"And how long will you be showing it today?"

The broker checked his watch. "Just as soon as the lass makes the trip through with her significant other, I'll be heading for the office. Total of two hours."

"That's moving them."

"Sell themselves, they do," the man agreed.

"I suppose your commission's negotiable?"

The man blinked, then smiled. "You suppose incorrectly, sir."

"Don't you have to split the commission with the buyer's agent?"

"That's true, sir. But whatever arrangement the buyer's agent makes with his client is his or her business. The seller listed this property with my firm, and my firm is very adamant about a full commission, particularly in the current seller's market, if you take my meaning."

"A seller's market."

"Quite so."

"Would the owner carry the paper?"

A little silence followed this question. Finally the broker said, "You must not be from around these parts."

Banerjhee raised an eyebrow. "That's true."

"And where would you be from, then, if I might inquire?"

Banerjhee gestured toward the street, and found himself readily . . . elaborating. "They've just brought me in. Normally, HR personnel and my wife would do the house-hunting. But what with my wife packing up in Anaheim and our son still in school, I thought I'd look around for myself. "

"Anaheim." The broker looked past him. "That would be headquarters for the outfit that bought out SynBad. Across the way, there."

"Indeed it would."

The broker's eyes glittered. "Heard they somewhat missed the biotech boat."

Well, well, thought Banerjhee. "That's precisely why we acquired SynBad. We've set things right with a single purchase."

"Yes?" the realtor replied mildly. "They're going down that road?"

"Full steam ahead."

The realtor patted his left shoulder with his right hand. "I saw on the news about a mouse. Had a human ear growing right out of its back." He pinched his left ear. "Full-size, like."

This pantomime engendered Banerjhee's first smile of the day. "You'd be amazed at what they're doing, across the street."

"Are you, across the street," the realtor's eyes darted to one side and the other, "publicly traded?"

"Oh yes," Banerjhee replied, as if confidentially. "The corporate name is Second Bounce, LLP."

The realtor clicked a ball point pen and made a note on the face of the prospectus atop a stack of them.

"Ticker symbol SBNC," Banerjhee added helpfully, turning his head to watch the man write.

"I'll tell you what." The realtor laid his pen precisely parallel to the spine of his book, halfway between it and a cellphone. "The owner seems interested in cash, though I can't wonder why. His new home makes this place look like a proper sty. At any rate, thirty percent down would get his attention. The financing, of course, would be up to you. You're pre-approved, I assume?"

"For a three and a half million dollar loan?" Banerjhee asked incredulously.

The realtor raised an eyebrow. Clearly he'd held the hand of a nervous buyer more than once. "If you've got the thirty percent in cash, which would be. . . ." He produced a calculator from the breast pocket of his suit jacket and punched in some numbers. The figure of one point one five million had already appeared in Banerjhee's mind, and he noted, as he always did, that the realtor's calculator was the sort that could only add, subtract, multiply and divide.

After a couple of deleted attempts the realtor read off the display, "One million forty-eight thousand and five hundred dollars. That's the downstroke. Plus various closing costs—the title search, inspections and so forth. If you've got that kind of cash, you could certainly get a conforming loan for the balance from almost any lender, and put yourself in the running for a close at very near the asking." He fingered the keys. "Rule of thumb, by the way, on a place like this—mortgage, insurance, maintenance, taxes and so forth?—it'll cost you about ten percent of your loan per year, which comes to a quarter of a million bucks, or twenty thousand three hundred eighty-seven dollars per month." The realtor tapped a decisive fingernail on the calculator display and winked at Banerjhee. "Ain't no hill for a high-stepper, as Robbie Burns liked to say, and a hell of an investment."

Banerjhee nodded distantly, with a slight smile, as if the realtor had solved a curious riddle for him. "I suppose he would say that, who so appreciated the doings of mice and men and, especially, women."

The realtor returned the calculator to his breast pocket. "Anything else I can help you with?"

Banerjhee asked for his business card.

Back across the street, he retrieved his van. The striped bar remained down at the security gate, and the guard asked him to wait. A few minutes later he returned with a clipboard and said, "Your name's on the list, Mr. Rolf. I must reclaim your parking permit before you can go."

"But Wycliff." He pointed at the windshield. "It's a decal."

Wycliff slipped a single-edge disposable razor blade from beneath the spring of the clipboard.

Banerjhee looked at it.

"Sorry, sir." The guard shrugged. "It's the job."

Banerjhee set about scraping the decal off the inside lower left corner of his windshield. Every so often he gathered the shavings off the dash and handed them through the window to Wycliff, who solicitously waited with cupped hand.

"You do this often?" Banerjhee asked, annoyed by the resistance of the last square centimeter of the sticker, too close to the dash to scrape easily.

"Not so much any more, sir," Wycliff answered, with a melancholy tone. "Everybody's accounted for, more or less. It's not been a happy scene around here."

Banerjhee handed over the last of the fragments. "Oh." He

plucked the realtor's business card from the passenger seat and crumpled it into the waiting hand. "If you wouldn't mind?"

"Not at all, Mr. Rolf." Wycliff inverted the hand over a wastebasket inside the kiosk, and Banerjhee handed him the razorblade. As Wycliff reclipped it to his board, he said, "I sometimes wonder how long I'm going to last myself."

"Never fear, Wycliff," Banerjhee assured the kindly guard. "This outfit is always going to be feeling the need for security."

"Yes, Sir." Wycliff permitted himself a little smile as he stepped back into the kiosk. The striped bar lifted through ninety degrees, and Wycliff touched his forehead with the side of his hand. "Good luck, Mr. Rolf."

FOUR

I think you should go."
Madja made a little face. "I want to."
"I'm glad you're going."
"What about you?"
He shrugged. "I'll probably starve to death."
She smiled and touched his face. "Are you hungry?"
He caught her hand. "Yes. Aren't you?"
"A little. Let me see what I can do.'
She made them a Caesar salad with lots of garlic. Banerjhee opened a bottle of wine, toasted croutons in olive oil, and filled a small pitcher with sparkling water, to which he added an orange slice. When all was ready, they sat opposite one another at the kitchen table and raised their glasses.
"Be sure Sam takes you to the Museum of Science and Industry," Banerjhee said. "They say it's fantastic."
"What about the Playboy mansion?"
Banerjhee frowned. "Isn't that in Los Angeles?"
"Oh, I," Madja laughed, "I really don't know."
Banerjhee laughed too.
"There's no place like this place," Madja assured him.
"As dingbat next door, there," Banerjhee moved his head toward Toby Pride's house, "told me a few days ago, if only mushrooms grew here, we could call this place Paradise."

"He needs a trip to Utar Pradesh." Madja arranged a napkin on her lap. "But why does he say that? Does he like *fungi* with his beer?"

"On his pizza, maybe," Banerjhee said. "But I think he is referring to *psilocibe mexicana,* also known as *Teonanácatl,* and various other species among the psychedelic *fungi.* I doubt he would be particular about which." Banerjhee poured water for each of them. "There's one whose range extends from the lower Olympic Peninsula to northern British Columbia, for example, called the Liberty Cap. *Psilocibe semi lanceata.* SA couple of those, properly dried, would take the top of Mr. Pride's head off." He measured two knuckles of his pinky finger with his thumb. "It's about this long, mucilaginous in texture, and resembles nothing so much as a small, circumcised penis."

"I know exactly what you're talking about."

"Hey."

"Not your ordinary toadstool."

"Far from it. Properly dried they're quite strong. The psychoactive ingredient is psilocybin. In large doses it can have debilitating side effects—speech impediments, tingling or numb extremities, stuff like that. Not unlike the tenants next door, they'll go away if you wait long enough."

Madja said, "Can we talk about something else?"

Banerjhee blinked twice. "Sure."

Madja studiedly set her fork astride her plate, placed both hands in her lap, and looked into her husband's eyes. "While in Chicago, I'm going to look for a job."

If an altimeter had hung on the wall nearby, Banerjhee would have reflexively checked it. His ears didn't pop, but his stomach experienced the effects of a precipitous change of altitude more like those attributable to the maneuvers of a crop duster than a tranquil suburban kitchen.

"You're the one who has always been of the opinion," Madja

reminded him, "that once you hit the California border, you might as well keep on going."

"It's . . . cold in Chicago," he said, cutting straight to the objective marrow.

"Hear me out."

"No," he said without force.

"This is for your own good."

"I feel plenty good just as I am."

"Banerjhee. . . ."

Banerjhee lay his fork astride his own plate, its salad untouched. Regarding the single anchovy atop it, he made the hapless observation that it may well have perished for insufficient cause.

Distressed, Madja said, "I should have waited until—"

"I'm listening," Banerjhee said to the fish.

"Very well," she said after a moment. "We'll be able to see Sam often. I'm sure it would take no convincing at all for him to take his Sunday meal with us. Think of it. We haven't seen him since he left."

"I didn't see a lot of him before he left," Banerjhee noted. "You didn't either. I think it troubles you more. When a woman sees her son grown into a man—"

"Oh, BJ," she snapped. "Don't hand me that twaddle."

Banerjhee smiled. "I was just stalling while I marshaled my wit."

"You have more than one," she said sternly. "Engage them."

Banerjhee nodded vaguely. "It's a shame to waste this meal."

"Well eat, then, while I talk. It's never stopped you before."

"True." Banerjhee took a sip of wine, smacked his lips, and took another. "Kowabunga," he said, holding the glass to the light. "Talk about your chemistry."

Madja glanced at her own glass as if just remembering it was there. She, too, took a modest sip. "It's very good," she agreed, setting down her glass. As Banerjhee opened his mouth to make a point, she said, "I'm sure you can buy California wines in Illinois."

"But—"

"And in Illinois, you might be able to better afford them."

"But Madja, that's not fair. I'm extremely frugal."

"BJ," she said firmly, "are you going to listen to me or are you going to sit there and babble about wine?"

"I'm listening, I'm listening." He took up his fork and dealt himself a bite of romaine. Despite his discomfort, or perhaps because of it, Madja's dressing tasted delicious. Cooking every evening for the two of them, for the three of them when they were three, or for three or four guests less and less often, gave Madja great pleasure in more ways than one, but prime among them was cooking's function as an antidote to her job. She was very good at both.

"Very well, then," she said. "I'm not going to start in on how we've lived in California all our lives, how we love California, how California has changed for the worse, and how we don't belong here any more."

"Good. I'm fed up with all of those subjects. But California's our home. We vote. We—"

"I've already made the point about Sam. Think of what it would mean to spend another three or four years close to our son, the only other person in the entire world who truly means something to us."

"If he goes to medical school at Northwestern or some place in Chicago, it could be ten or twelve years," Banerjhee gloomily agreed. "Little bird, are you certain that Sam wants us to be so conspicuous in his life?"

"Of course he does. He knows that family is important, and we're all he has. We all have only each other. And besides, what's conspicuous about having Sunday lunch with your parents? The rest of the time he'll be too busy to see us. We'll move your library to Chicago intact. I'll find a job at least as interesting as the one I have now, and likely more so."

"Okay. What about–"

"Don't worry, I'm not about to do his laundry and clean his apartment. Sam won't end up living with us, either. You may, however," she reminded him, "have to coach him with his organic chemistry." Madja now tasted her own salad. "He asked something about Mendeleyev."

"Ah," Banerjhee brightened. "The Periodic Table. Now there was a stroke."

Daintily chewing she added, "Helping Sam with his studies would give you nothing but pleasure."

"I could make him the best chemist in Chicago."

"No doubt. And it would give you something to think about besides neutron stars and that bozo next door."

"So we're not going to leave neutron stars behind, along with bozo, mild winters, and the high cost of living?"

"Of course not. Think of it. Maybe you could audit courses in astrophysics at the Fermi Institute."

Banerjhee smiled.

"In any case, neutron stars will always be there. Yes? No?"

"Well, that depends, but as a rule they last about 4 million years."

"Good. Because there's a more important point. This house," she pointed her fork downward, "is worth a lot of money."

Banerjhee bit his lip. Here came the truth.

"We can sell this place, move everything to Chicago–"

"Except the garden," Banerjhee reminded her.

"Except the garden," Madja agreed. "The garden is going to have to stay here."

"It snows in Chicago," Banerjhee said glumly.

"Haven't you heard about global warming?"

"I have, but Chicago hasn't. Chicago plays basement table tennis some six months out of the year. Chicago consumes lots of football. And ice hockey. It's. . . ." He nodded with conviction. "It's a cruel and primitive environment."

"BJ," she insisted patiently, "we can sell this place, pay off what's left of the mortgage, and make an obscene profit. With no capitol gains unless we make over $500,000–five hundred thousand dollars!–we'll move lock, stock and library to Chicago, buy a place every bit this size and every bit this comfortable at half the price, gift it to Sam via a deed of trust–"

"That's my girl," Banerjhee smiled.

". . .And furnish it as we like," she continued. "We'll buy a modest little car that likes snow and ice, and we'll still distribute two or even three hundred thousand dollars among various fiduciary instruments. No matter what he pursues, Sam's education will be assured. No longer will there be worries about where the next plane ticket is going to come from. There will be no necessity to buy plane tickets, really."

"Except to fly to Baja or Florida or Hawaii," he pointed out. "Someplace warm."

"So," she said, "buy plane tickets to warm places. Gone will be the temptation to dip into the equity in our home to buy a new car or remodel the bathroom or do the things we need or would like to do. My paycheck will no longer be mainly servicing a mortgage. And you–" she pointed the fork at him, and Banerjhee feinted a glance over his shoulder, as if he weren't the you to whom she referred "–my ever-loving husband, will never have to worry about being out of a job again. You can pursue astrophysics to your heart's content."

She was talking sense, as usual. Banerjhee had been out of work for over a year. Madja's job as head bookkeeper for a fifty-employee PR firm stood them in good stead, the house payments were relatively low with only seven years left to pay off, and Sam was getting about a 30% ride on books and tuition from his college. Still, Banerjhee often brooded over

36

why he'd been remaindered before his time. He understood that his former company had been brought down by a corporate raider. He'd come to terms with the fact that profit motive had destroyed any number of things he thought were more important, and he had faith that the legal attack on SynBad's historic entitlements would fail. But he could not come to terms with the fact that he'd been unable to find another job in his field. 'Ageism' only partially explained it. He was very good at what he did and commanded a range of knowledge that not only far exceeded pharmacology, but also complemented it.

What Madja had said about the culture changing around them, however, was true. He'd been to any number of Human Resource department interviews at any number of biotech companies, as well as chemistry and pharmaceutical labs. He'd even tried to get the state forensic crime lab to take him on. But they wanted to see an advanced degree quite different from the three he had earned, and he could not convince them to give him a chance; for he was confident that if the job involved chemistry, physics, mathematics, or biology, he would quickly master any tasks entrusted to him. In fact, as Banerjhee explained to the interviewer, there was little he'd fancy more than a chance to analyze one of the Unabomber's home-made blasting caps. The Human Resource Person looked at him for a long moment, then assured Banerjhee that he'd keep his resumé in a special place. Again with the round file, Banerjhee reflected wryly, as the pebbled glass doors of laboratory after laboratory fell away on either side of him, in the long corridor to the exit.

Finally he took his resumé to a headhunter. This individual invited him to be seated while he examined Banerjhee's file, which he studied for a long time. The wall behind the desk displayed a photo of the headhunter in a red and white pineapple shirt and khaki shorts with his hand on the dorsal fin of a huge blue marlin, suspended upside down from a meathook hook over an unpainted and weatherbeaten wooden dock.

When the headhunter had finished his perusal of Banerjhee's resumé, he stood up as if to stretch and paced to the office door. There he took a casual look up and down the hallway, closed the door, and returned to his desk. He twice tapped Banerjhee's papers with a fingertip and said, "This is an admirable record of education and employment."

What was Banerjhee to say to that?

The headhunter turned a page. "When you turned fifty, you had a routine physical examination. Flexible sigmoidoscopy and all that."

"Quite the experience."

The headhunter didn't smile. "The EKG turned up a heart murmur."

"So it did."

"You had no idea?"

"None."

"No ill effects?"

"None."

"That's good. This was when?" The headhunter ran a finger down the top sheet.

"About five years ago."

"...Eight years ago," the headhunter said, stopping the finger at a figure.

"Really?"

The headhunter turned a page, then another, then turned back and asked, "You've had no physical since?"

Banerjhee said nothing. Finally he shrugged.

"All right." The headhunter closed the file. "Does your wife work?"

"Yes."

"Good company? Benefits? Like, good insurance?"

"Very good."

"It covers you, of course."

"It covers me."

"That's good. Because you're in the gap."

"The . . . gap?"

"Yes, yes," the headhunter said impatiently. "The uninsurable gap between fifty-five, when you either can't afford insurance or no insurer will cover you, and sixty-three, when Medicare kicks in."

"I suppose that's so," Banerjhee admitted.

"Tell your wife to keep her job."

That's none of your goshdarned business, Banerjhee said to himself.

The headhunter closed Banerjhee's file. "As for you, Mr. Rolf, and this is off the record, no insurance carrier is going to allow a company whose employees it covers to hire you. You're a man of a certain age with a heart murmur which, minor as the latter may be, places you into a category of expense risk that far eclipses the value of any services you might conceivably render a company in the few productive years remaining before your retirement. *Capiche?*" He slid the resumé across the desk. "Save your money, don't hire my firm to place you, and you didn't hear it from me." The headhunter stood, rounded his desk, opened the door, and extended his hand. "Good luck, Mr. Rolf."

He taught a semester of night classes in organic chemistry at UC Davis. He enjoyed teaching, too, but in a qualified way, for most of the students, even the advanced ones, took his instruction for remedial purposes, desperate to pass so they could pursue a higher education in some lucrative vocation like plastic surgery or whatever. None of them was passionate about chemistry *per se.* On top of that the commute was nerve-wracking and expensive, and the pay was no good. In the end the university solved his discomfort for him by

39

shutting down their entire ancillary class program for lack of funding. From then on, students were expected to take their remedial courses via the internet.

Banerjhee liked computers just fine. Back when the personal computer was young, he'd written an essay defending it as a tool of great potential, as opposed to a harbinger of a restrictive and conformist society. He might have to rethink that one. In the meantime his once-formidable programming skills in Fortran, Pascal, and Basic had become superannuated. Try as he might, Banerjhee couldn't relate to the internet, not for teaching at any rate, nor for research. Depth and scope remained the purview of libraries, books, and journals. He did like the internet for buying books and browsing NASA's extremely cool library of Hubble images, but that was about it.

"What about you?" he said quietly. "You wouldn't have to work either."

Madja said, "Work is a good thing for somebody like me, BJ, and while I'm enjoying it less and less, I'm going to keep on working until it's time for you to retire and/or become eligible for Medicare."

Banerjhee didn't like to hear this, an unpleasant truth born of necessity, but he said nothing.

"Besides," Madja added, "what would I do without working in Chicago? Sit around with you talking about neutron stars?"

"What's wrong with neutron stars?" Banerjhee asked plaintively. "Would you rather discuss the Chicago Cubs?"

"Nothing's wrong with either one of them," Madja replied, "except the Cubs don't win very much, I'm told." She smiled as Banerjhee shook his head. "And now that you mention it, I'd rather listen to you talk about neutron stars than anybody at all about basketball."

"Baseball," Banerjhee laughed. "I think."

"Baseball, basketball—they're all the same. Organized sports pave the road to fascism." This was Madja's favorite summation of the world-wide and historically deep craving for stadium sports. "The guy who wrote that wound up becoming a Christian," she added, beating Banerjhee to his usual retort.

"Out of despair, no doubt," he replied, easily parroting her own standard rejoinder. And they both began to giggle. Banerjhee extended his hand across the table and took one of hers. "As if I could live without you while you lived in Chicago," he said tenderly.

"I knew you would listen to reason. And in just the nick of time," she said with a smile, "as, I'm sure I have to remind you, I'm taking the redeye on Friday night."

"Friday night?" It took two or three seconds. When the realization arrived, Banerjhee's smile converted to a mask of panic. "But that's tonight."

"You've known about it since Tuesday," Madja smiled. "You've had all week to get used to the idea." She pushed back her chair and stood up. "If you wouldn't mind doing the dishes, I can start packing."

He'd long since become used to his wife's decision-making process. It appeared impulsive, to say the least, but that was hardly the case. Madja thought long and hard and with unusual clarity about a problem, rarely consulting an outside opinion until after her mind was made up; at which point attempts at dissuasion were arduous at best and rarely successful. Banerjhee took a contemplative sip of wine. In fact, he had learned to rely on the rigor of her thought. But he could see this Chicago business was going to set some records for whiplash.

"Uh," he said, "how long did we plan for you to be gone?"

"Two weeks."

"Two weeks?" He made no attempt to conceal his dismay. "I agreed to two weeks? What about your job? What about me?"

"Upon my return I expect to have a new job in place. The present job owes me two weeks' vacation, seven sick days, and four personal days. I am also owed two weeks' unpaid leave. I'll give them notice when all of that has been consumed. In the meantime you and I will spend the balance of the year enjoying the sunset of our California sojourn. With proper planning and a lot of cardboard boxes, we should be in Chicago in time for Christmas goose with Sam."

"Goose," Banerjhee said happily. But then, "Packing furniture, putting the house to rights, getting it on the market, deciding what to take, what to leave behind. . . . Yes," he sighed. "It sounds most restful."

"By the time I return," Madja assured him, "we'll both be looking forward to the adventure."

Banerjhee took a final sip of wine and set the unfinished glass aside. "Two weeks," he said thoughtfully. "It seems like forever."

"So it does." Madja smiled sweetly. "Any last requests?"

FIVE

The canopy of light cast by the bigger cities was behind him, which left the sky black and shot with stars. The drive back from the Oakland airport on 580 was a long one, however, with its strong potential for introspection obliterated by the density of traffic. National Public Radio was a feckless mumble of human interest rendered sentimental by cheesy sound effects. The record spinner at the jazz station was on a big band kick too aggressive for Banerjhee's state of mind. Every other spot on the dial having been colonized by homogenization, he turned the radio off.

Would he miss California? Certainly. He missed it already. He'd missed it for a long time. California had changed beyond recognition in Banerjhee's lifetime. Yet the air between midnight and dawn, the tangerine sunsets, a full moon over the San Francisco Bay, the splash of a jumping fish in a Delta channel at dusk, the sussurant clatter of a eucalyptus grove, the impossibly thick dew attributable to impossibly thick fog, dew which dripped from dawn eves and tree limbs as if it had been raining all night, and hundreds of other details retained slivers of definition that summed to the synecdoche of Banerjhee Rolf's California. His mind wandered freely among them.

He remembered a scientist who had visited the Farallones Islands trying to figure out how the wind there could blow thirty knots while the islands remained enshrouded by impenetrable fog.

He remembered the old drunk in a threadbare pea jacket who spent his days sipping beer out of a paper sack in a laundromat on Polk Street, who wore the merchant marine pin in the shape of a clipper ship, which meant that he'd rounded Cape Horn under the canvas of a square rigger—a clipper ship: think of it! He remembered, too, that one day the old-timer wasn't there, and Banerjhee never saw him again.

And what about the paradisical vision to be had when surmounting Echo Summit and Carson Pass, several thousand feet up and heading west out of the gray alkali of Nevada into the russet and green of late summer Sierra Nevada threaded by purling freshets of thirty-five-degree glacial runoff? The soul lured west, not east. Never east.

Or the luminous spiral he'd watched uncoil in the sky over the hills of Menlo Park while sitting under a California oak, late one night, early one morning, some forty years before. The spiral turned out to have been a kind of Coriolis effect on the exhaust contrail of a rocket launched by the Navy, way down the coast. But in the inexplicable moment the wraith pixelated green and blue and yellow and took up a quarter of the night sky, straight up. One of the most beautiful things Banerjhee had ever seen, he'd hoped in the moment that it might have been a uniquely manifested astral event; except, of course, the spiral was just too big. And it dispersed long before dawn.

Even then Banerjhee knew that, of perhaps six supernovae observed throughout history in our own galaxy, at least one, noted by observers in China and North America in the 11th century, was visible in broad daylight for twenty-three days, but took up no more space in the sky than the breadth of a man's hand. One result of this galactic cataclysm was the Crab Nebula, host to NP0531, one of the first pulsars discovered. A pulsar is a rapidly rotating neutron star—some 30 times per second in this case—and, just here, Banerjhee tried to interdict himself from the pleasurable mulling of the many interesting theoretical implications of a star equivalent to possibly three solar masses compacted by gravitational collapse to a ball about six miles across, spinning like a top, whose outer shell is solid iron. . . . But the interdiction failed. In fact the whole scenario had and would always fascinate and terrify Banerjhee, comparing favorably in his mind with putting a tongue depressor in the devil's mouth and asking him to say ah-h-h-h.

The line of thought led to another of his fascinations with celestial objects, that as one observes a supernova, for example, not to mention most gleams in the night sky, one is observing an event that actually happened a long, long, long time ago, some sixty-five hundred years in the case of the Crab Nebula. This idea had fomented in a young Banerjhee's mind the poetic notion that in standing beneath a night sky an observer is in fact witnessing a kind of chronological simultaneity, a snapshot of events separated by hundred, thousands, perhaps billions of years. That one can experience a similar effect in observing ambient geology, or butterflies in various stages of development, or blooms and bulbs and shoots, and the compost pile in one's garden didn't seem to Banerjhee to add up to quite the same dramatic effect. One's garden might represent ten year's work, or, by the species of its various denizens, eons of survival and evolution. The structure of a tree fern, for example, precedes the ice age. Much of a night sky is much older than anything you can find on earth, but it's *right now,* too. So it had always been possible for Banerjhee to convince himself, for an idle hour anyway, that he was witnessing it all happening at once, without Time.

The description of that test rocket's spiraling exhaust became the basis of Banerjhee's mathematics thesis, and his sense of the wonders to be encountered via curiosity had never left him. The study of neutron stars, which is a lot of nuclear physics, mathematics, astronomy, general relativity, quantum mechanics, magnetism, chemistry, imagination—all very interesting, depending upon one's turn of mind—seemed just another logical extension of Banerjhee's curiosity about the things going on everywhere he turned . . . in California.

The inexplicable congestion on a busy freeway, for example, which slows traffic to a crawl and ties it into a knot for no discernible reason—no big rig overturned next to the road, no tragedy on the other side of the median, no mattress in lane four or pothole crew blocking lane one; just a lump into which traffic slows and out of which it accelerates. The lump itself can travel forward or backward, as Banerjhee conjectured, though he'd never heard anybody say so. Surely somebody was modeling the problem? Surely it would be found to touch on elements of chaos theory? Someday, maybe, automobiles equipped with fuzzy logic circuits, making countless minute corrections too rapid and sophisticated for their human drivers, could avoid such congestion? Maybe, maybe knot. Haha. Hahaha. Hahaha. . . .

The bad pun almost cheered him, despite the certainty of Madja's two-week absence. He didn't like any time without her. Though deep in concentration in his garage library, his ears would prick up like a dog's when the car pool dropped her off at the mailbox, and from that moment his day started over. He would already have shopped for the fresh ingredients she would require. And after she'd taken a half-hour or so to change her clothes and freshen up, maybe even take a quick nap, they would meet in the kitchen. There he kept their drinks fresh while she herded cuisine and they chatted about the day's events.

"If a star the size of the sun were to collapse to its constituent neutrons. . . ." he might say.

"Andrea had her baby," Madja would counter. "That leaves Mark the only experienced hand in Payroll."

". . .the resulting object would have a diameter of twenty-two feet."

"The revamped so-called budget forgot to allow for paid part-time help. One unpaid intern isn't. . . ."

". . .With a density of hundreds of billions of tons per cubic inch. Think of it."

". . .sufficient for the duration of her maternity leave. Three months! And who knows if she'll come back?"

"If this kitchen were on its surface and you jumped off the countertop, you'd hit the floor at two million miles per hour!"

Madja laughed aloud, and Banerjhee joined her, adding, "Spilling your delicious Sonoma Zinfandel."

"Is this the same one we had last week?"

"No. You didn't like that one. This is a new one. Only a dollar more. Do you like it?"

"Very much."

"Oh, well. We'll get a case."

"I thought we were going back to drinking in France."

"Not until they get their politics straightened out."

"Banerjhee, stop it!"

"Just kidding. These Oregon Pinots are delicious, but they're expensive. Next week we'll revisit Hermitage. Or Bordeaux."

"I wouldn't care if we never left California," she would say, her back turned as she worked and talked, the tapes of her apron tied in a bow at the small of her back.

"I hear that. . . ." Banerjhee spoke softly, aloud, to the light-streaked windshield, repeating what he'd said at the time, now wondering at the ironic coloration her off-hand remark about California wines assumed in retrospect. It seemed like a false sentiment. Had it been a fib? A lie? The repartee had taken place not so long ago. Surely by then she'd been contemplating what from now on he would always refer to, in the matter of Madja Rolf vs The State of California, as the Chicago Decision?

Up 680 the traffic lightened somewhat, but the incidental light suffused throughout the night sky seemed only to increase. Forty years ago, out here, Banerjhee and everybody else could clearly see the Milky Way, the edge-wise view of our home galaxy. Now it's invisible, obscured by an atmosphere polluted by light and other things. Time was, out here, come to think of it, this highway didn't even exist. Or, if it did exist, it was two lanes of blacktop, or even one lane of dirt. This reminded Banerjhee that, when he was in college, most of the megalopolis through which he was now driving had been orchards. And that reminded him of an old man who told him of climbing a cottonwood every afternoon for most of July and August, as a boy on the outskirts of Fresno, late in the nineteenth century. His father posted him there to watch the road for the ox-drawn wagon that would have hauled his father's brother with his family all the way from St. Louis. And one afternoon, by golly, it showed up.

Banerjhee found himself re-circling a body of thought he'd visited before, usually involuntarily, which always boiled down to the same question: Could it be that he'd run his time on earth? Was he going to expend a greater and greater portion of his day bitching about the changes wrought all round him throughout his lifetime, until his pleasure in life dwindled to zilch? Is this what it meant to get old? As in, hey man, your grousing about freeway congestion is getting really *old.* Turn on the radio.

Well, his mind quickly replied, there's nothing on the radio tonight. In Chicago, will it be worse? All the radio stations are owned by the same handful of companies, and if you have any doubt about that, all you need do is scan the dial. You'll hear the same music up and down it. Music generated by factories pandering to a narrow demographic that completely eschews the like of Banerjhee, whether he's young enough to be included in it or not. Do you have to be of a certain age to appreciate hitting a linoleum floor at two million miles an hour?

He grunted, amused but not amused. Of the few friends he'd cultivated, or who had cultivated Madja and himself, for they had to include Madja or Banerjhee wasn't interested, and *vice versa,* all had dissipated, harvested by a unilateral interest in golf or poker or Hollywood movies, by age and mortality, by California's economic tribulations. His peers had all quit, retired, or been fired. Many among them had taken untenured academic positions in small, far-flung university towns. And, aside from the not-negligible fact that Banerjhee's devotion to his job made a pretty boring person of himself, his closest friends, the ones that dated from his days in college and graduate school, were, almost without exception, dead or disappeared, culled by jobs in Australia or Europe but also by suicide, two or three overdoses, alcoholism—which latter two he had always considered as slow forms of suicide—Vietnam, car and train and airline crashes, a sailboat vanished into thin air during a circumnavigation, death in childbirth, an unsolved murder at an Interstate rest stop, even a pilot who cracked up a stunt plane. These and other obituaries had thinned the interesting characters from his life, those to whom he need explain very little, those to whom he didn't mind listening for hours, those among them of reliable, i.e. not tricky, drinking companions. Gone. Most of them didn't rate an obituary their family didn't have to pay the newspaper for, as his own wouldn't, and he wondered about that, too. Every other day it seemed the *San*

Francisco Chronicle and the *New York Times* featured a long obituary, often with a picture, of some actor or TV personality or movie star of whom Banerjhee had never heard, and he had to wonder what these people had possibly done on earth to warrant this emphatic if admittedly ephemeral notice. Certainly they meant nothing to him, or to his wife, and maybe even to people who watched a lot of TV. The practice seemed deliberately designed to inculcate into readers of newspapers insidious insecurities regarding their truant consumption of the greatest propaganda machine ever deployed. Yes? No?

That was one way to fathom it. And fathomed that way, the logic of the story became funereal indeed. The way the government encouraged people to think that the attacks on New York City of September 11, 2001, came out the blue, for example, out of nowhere, without ideology, cause, or justification, that they were some kind of jealous prank perpetrated by illiterate cowards envious of America's world eminence and so forth. Could it be that the day would come when he could be arrested for committing such thoughts to paper or, more subversive, to a never-to-be-anonymous-if-the-government-has-anything-to-say-about-it email?

In the year since his forced retirement, he had discovered many pleasures. He could read about neutron stars to his heart's content, he could ruminate the calculations of his betters and predecessors for days on end, he could meticulously forage for the best cook he'd ever known, he could ignore television to the extent of not even having one in his house, and he could cultivate his garden, but he could not forgo the dubious discipline of reading two newspapers five days a week on the grounds that, for better or worse, they kept him somewhat informed.

If, as Jacques Ellul—the same guy who made the crack about organized sports, whose name Madja could never remember, and one of the Unabomber's favorite thinkers—pointed out as obvious, that without mass media there can be no propaganda, if this were indisputably true and never more so, then Thomas Jefferson or somebody had also reminded whoever was listening that without newspapers there can be no freedom of thought. The problem as Banerjhee saw it was that mass media—television and radio—were ascendant, and that newspapers, whose circulations have been circling the drain for fifty or sixty years, hardly came into the equation any more, let alone into the definition of mass media. The masses don't read newspapers, and therefore it doesn't make any difference to them what newspapers report or opine, and it's that simple. The masses get their information from television, and television is a corporate entity, by default at least partly if not wholly a government organ, which fact is more slithery than a pelagic Ouroboros because more than ever American government is a corporate organ, a-and, and corporations know only one Good, which is their own Good and none other.

Banerjhee realized with a start that he was parked in his own driveway, that the Peugeot's engine was still idling, and that its headlights were illuminating the primer-spotted back doors of his own Econoline.

He was holding his breath and his heart was racing. He exhaled loudly and so forcefully that a nimbus of condensation appeared on the inside of the windshield. He inhaled slowly and deeply, exhaled likewise, and did it again. He switched off the motor and killed the lights. With a little more measured breathing his heart rate slowed, and a certain tightness in his chest relaxed. I've got to stop reading those damn newspapers, he said to himself, or at least learn to discipline my mind not to worry about them so much. My weekend moratorium on news is no longer sufficient. They're power tools too after all, those newspapers, just like their bastard spawn, the television. And they're going to give me cancer, or a heart attack, or a

51

nervous breakdown. He let his forehead down onto the rim of steering wheel between his two hands which still gripped it. What in the world must the insides of the heads of those who watch television day in and day out be like? It's terrifying to contemplate. What did that doctor say about the woman in Florida who had been on life support for 13 years? That her cranial cavity was filled mostly with fluid? It must be true. He had read it in a newspaper.

"I must break that habit," he implored the Peugeot horn button.

He straightened up and had just managed a second long, centering sigh when something impacted the driver's door with a loud thump. The noise startled him, but when he turned to see what caused it, he jumped at the sight of the hands and tear-streaked face of a woman, pressed against the window. Her features were so distorted that it took him a few seconds to recognize the woman to whom Toby Pride had introduced him on Tuesday afternoon. "Mr. BJ," she implored. But from inside the car her plea was muffled and incoherent. Outside the car it may have been, too. She emphatically slapped her hand against the window, and a ring on her finger made a loud snap against the glass, inches from Banerjhee's face. He tried to open the door but she was slumped against it. Finally he rolled down the window.

"Yes, dear." He did not remember her name. "What's the trouble?"

"He–he w-wanted. . . ." The girl reached through the window with both hands and clung to his neck. "Oh, Mr. BJ. He watches those porn movies. He–he. . . ." She dissolved into sobs, her head on his shoulder.

Banerjhee wasn't particularly taken aback at this small revelation, but he was pretty sure it wasn't any of his business. "Certainly if. . . ." he began tentatively. "Have you been. . . ? I mean . . . against your. . . ?"

"We were just about to get in the hot tub," she whimpered. "And he—he is like totally out of control."

"Who, Toby? Out of control? Let me out of the car." But the girl wouldn't turn him loose. Her hair smelled of suntan oil and marijuana and cigarettes and other things he only involuntarily recognized. Banerjhee pried himself away from her, slid across the front seat, and let himself out by the passenger door. When he'd come around the back of the car to the driver's side, he saw that, except for a pair of athletic socks, and a finely linked gold chain around her waist, the woman was completely naked. Nevertheless he gingerly took her into his arms, ever the humanitarian. She folded herself into his embrace, her reactive plaint putting him in mind of nothing so much as a loudly complaining cat who, being taken up out of sympathy, immediately begins to purr because it thinks it has found its person.

"There, there," he said. "I'm sorry. . . . What was your name?"

"Esme," the girl responded with disconcerting immediacy. "It's short for Esmerelda."

"A nice name," Banerjhee assured her, at a loss for meaningful banter. "Does it . . . um, hurt?"

"No," she said forcefully, "not particularly. It's just that he didn't have *permission,* the son of a bitch."

"Permission to. . . ?"

"Permission to—to—" She shouted and stamped a bare foot on one of Banerjhee's shoes. "All he had to do was be *nice* to me. . . ." She looked down. "Excuse me. Did that hurt?"

Well, yes, Banerjhee thought, mindful of the impression this scene might make with his neighbors—a naked girl after midnight with Madja out of town, and so forth. Well then, this should be none of my business. He offered the young woman his jacket.

"Won't you talk to him, Mr. BJ?" she tearfully implored,

not donning the coat but clutching its lapels between her breasts. "He's got to learn some manners. Don't you think? Don't you? You have manners. Where did you get them?"

"Let's back up. You're talking about Toby?"

"Yes. Yes, of course I'm talking about Toby. Who do you think I'm talking about? Junipero Serra?"

"Well—no," Banerjhee said, trying not to laugh. "Not Junipero Serra."

"Well, you're right, Mr. BJ, I—"

"Banerjhee."

She blinked. "What?"

"That's my name."

"Toby told me it was BJ."

"No," he said patiently, "it's Banerjhee. Spelt B-a-n-e-r, pronounced banner. . . ."

"Banner," she said, wiping her cheeks with two fingertips.

"J-h-e-e, pronounced gee, as in whiz."

"Gee," she smiled. "As in whiz."

"Banerjhee."

"Banner-gee-whiz," she repeated faithfully, and sniffled.

"Thank you," he said. "I think."

"I'm sorry," she said sincerely. "I'm usually pretty good with names."

"Better than you are with boyfriends, I hope."

"Oh," she smiled, "Toby's not a bad man. Sometime's he's just an impetuous butthole, is all."

"What makes a man impetuous is your butthole," said a third voice.

They turned to find Toby Pride standing in his own driveway, which ran parallel to Banerjhee's. Except for an English rugby scarf, sunglasses, a Greek fisherman's cap worn backwards, and a pair of red cowboy boots, Pride was naked too.

"Don't talk like that in front of the neighbors," Esme stage-whispered, articulating perhaps the foremost among Banerjhee's thoughts.

"Toby," Banerjhee said, "can't you have your fun without hurting people?"

"Or insulting them?" the girl put in.

"But BJ, dude. . . ." Toby protested, waving off the chastisement. "Cut me some slack."

"What?" Banerjhee replied, somewhat exasperated. "Why?"

"Because, dude–" Toby spread his hands. "I won the lottery!"

SIX

"Liar! You did not!" shouted Esme, with unexpected energy. "You did not win the fucking lottery. You got about that much money." She held up a thumb and forefinger about an inch apart. "And it's not much bigger than your—"

"Then how come it hurt so much?" Pride interrupted her.

"It's not a question of hurt!" She stamped her foot. "Ow!"

"Now boy, now girl," Banerjhee protested, "let's. . . ." He stopped. Let's what? "How about let's all go inside, get dressed, and be friends."

"I'll go for the last two," Pride pouted.

"You call that a choice? I like being outside, naked, and friendless." Esme folded her hands under her breasts. "Look at my choices."

"Nice." Pride suddenly became reasonable. "BJ's right, honey. Let's all go inside and be friends."

"Banerjhee," Esme said.

"How's that?"

"His name's Banerjhee."

Toby frowned. "What kind of name is that?"

"His name."

"Really?" Toby looked at Banerjhee as if the latter had betrayed him.

57

Banerjhee wished he'd never brought it up, but, "Yes," he affirmed. "That's my name."

Esme taught Toby how to pronounce it. When he'd gotten a passable version going, she rewarded him with a chaste little kiss. In return Toby put a consoling arm over her shoulders and told her she didn't have to get dressed if she didn't want to.

"Hmph." Esme supplemented her minimal ensemble with a frown. "A lousy $45,000 and you think you're king of the world."

"You're the queen of my world," Pride tried.

She moved her chin. "It's not even a down payment on a house."

Pride cheerfully regarded his home as they walked up the driveway. "It would be if we moved to . . . ahm, if we moved to. . . ."

"Chicago," Banerjhee suggested.

"Too cold," Toby disagreed. "But hey," he pointed out cheerfully, "who wants to settle down? Think of something else to spend it on."

"But you don't even work," Esme protested, as if poaching the thought straight from Banerjhee's head. "It's not fair."

"What do you mean I don't work?" Pride countered testily. "You think that gun-toting blowmonkey arbitrage isn't work?"

Ah so, Banerjhee thought, my perspicacious wife.

"No," Esme replied. "I think it's a game to you, haggling in pidgin Spanish with people who would just as soon kill you as do business with you."

"At least I know where they stand," Pride retorted.

"What's *that* supposed to mean. . . ?"

As Banerjhee watched his neighbors, both of them quite naked, stroll arm in arm up the driveway past the black BMW, arguing about drug dealing as casually as if they'd just come in from an evening walk, he could not help but notice Esme's pulchritudinous behind, emphasized by radically thin tanlines, particularly as it was juxtaposed with Toby's, which model itself was surprisingly muscular on a guy who did nothing but sit on it. Banerjhee eschewed this latter observation like a barn swallow narrowly missing an overhanging eve, however, and recontemplating Esme's behind he unaccountably recalled a stipulation, encountered in his studies, that a marshmallow, falling to the surface of a neutron star, would impact it with the explosive power of a World War II atomic bomb.

"Hey, BJ," Toby said over his shoulder. "Come in and have a beer with us." When Banerjhee obviously hesitated, Pride added, "It's okay. The fight's over." He brushed Esme's hair with the flat of his hand. "Isn't it, honey."

"Don't touch me," she said with no particular emphasis.

"Mmmmm." Pride licked her shoulder. "Salty. C'mon, B.J. We'll have some fun. Relax a little bit. Maybe take a hot tub."

Banerjhee couldn't imagine anything more nerve-wracking than getting into a steaming hot tub with anybody, let alone these two. "Thank you, Toby, but it's way past my bedtime."

Esme turned on her heel, handed Banerjhee's jacket to Toby, and marched back down the driveway. If Banerjhee had been a cat, he'd soon have been peering out from under the rocker panel of the BMW, suspiciously and out of reach. "Oh, Sweetie," Esme said, taking the reluctant Banerjhee's arm. "You were so nice to me, just now, and so considerate when I was having my little moment. Won't you come in and teach Toby some manners?"

Banerjhee smiled. "I haven't got all night."

"C'mon," she laughed, "Toby's not so bad. And I'm not either," she added.

Unable to restrain a long-suffering sigh, which Esme appeared or affected not to notice, Banerjhee walked up to

Pride's house, arm in arm with Esme. The neighbors would just have to shift for themselves.

They passed through the garage, where Banerjhee noticed a severely customized Harley-Davidson, teal with black pinstriping and a few chromed accessories, a machine he'd not even known that Pride owned. He'd never heard its engine, and, noting its two straight pipes, it was almost inconceivable that he wouldn't hear it. If Pride had never fired it up, Banerjhee had reason to be grateful. Against the wall stood a bright red sheet-metal mechanic's credenza on casters, its trays and a couple of open drawers packed with end and box and torque wrenches, ratchets and sockets, screwdrivers, Allen keys, and so forth. The tools, he could see, were obviously brand-new, unscratched, non-greasy, and perhaps, like the motorcycle, never used. A bicycle hung upside down, from a pair of hooks screwed to a tie rafter, above a brand-new washer and dryer. The bike frame was alloy with exotic derailleurs, stirrup pedals, and shock-absorbing forks—another undoubtedly expensive toy. This too he'd never seen before, but he thought he was getting the picture. Toby Pride had money and expensive, redneck taste, but he didn't really know what to do with either one of them, and maybe Banerjhee had been sent by fate to talk him into making a large donation to The Nature Conservancy.

The kitchen manifested a quality inverse to that of the toys in the garage. The sink, full of dishes, emanated a pungency of mildew, deteriorating food, and damp cigarette ashes. The linoleum was cracked and bubbled. Empty pizza boxes were stacked on a table in a small dining area through which the trio passed before they filed into a darkened living room.

Here Banerjhee was confronted with his notion of a feckless antechamber to Nowhere. On the floor to the left of the entry door two televisions flickered adjacent to each other, opposite a couch. One had lost its signal altogether and displayed only snow. It may have been wired to a VCR that stood on edge next to it, whose lights were blinking. Scan lines climbed slowly up the glass face of the other set, rippling over some kind of comedy or drama taking place in a kitchen whose sterility was the inverse of Toby and Esme's kitchen, in flat pastel colors. Another VCR and a tall shelf unit full of CDs and tapes and stereo equipment stood beyond, emitting barely audible music which Banerjhee didn't know enough to call trance. It sounded exceptionally meaningless to him, but after a few minutes he reluctantly noted a slightly compelling lack of urgency to the sound, like maybe everybody still had all week to get to the air-raid shelter before nothing mattered anymore. There wasn't a book in sight.

Esme threw a TV Guide and two pillows onto the floor by way of clearing off the couch. "Sit down, sit." Banerjhee politely took a seat.

Toby paused in front of the televisions. A nimbus of light, diffracted by his body hair, traced his silhouette. "What's your pleasure, dude? We got it all, pretty much." A cellphone began to chime God Bless America. "Take care of BJ, Esme," Pride said, looking around. "Where in the fuck. . . ?"

Esme stood directly in front of Banerjhee, hands on hips. "There's two or three flavors of beer. Wine, I think there's some white left, plenty of red, all kinds of whiskey and such." She snapped her fingers. "You like martinis? I make a killer martini."

"Oh, really?" Banerjhee said mildly, struggling to stay afloat in the bottomless sofa.

"Yep. Been a bartender since I was in college."

"You . . . went to college?"

"Sure. The Fullerton Academy of Mixology. I worked as a stripper to pay my way. Oh! Maybe you know the place where I worked?" She knelt in front of him. "Fred's. Right down the road from John Wayne International? Real friendly girls.

Not too uptight about the hands-on stuff, but Fred never lets it go too far. In a whole year I never saw a fight. It's been there forever."

"I haven't been south of San Jose in a long time," Banerjhee smiled. "A martini would be ideal. Thank you."

She put a hand on each of his knees and leaned into his face. Again, though far from unpleasant, the proximity of her hair brought with it a kind of olfactory ship's log. "Vodka or gin?"

"Vodka. Very dry, very cold."

"Any particular flavor?"

"Of vodka? The cheaper the better, I'm sure."

"Shaken or stirred, my man?"

"Shaken, of course," Banerjhee stipulated demurely.

Esme sprang up with the ebullience of a young girl—which after all, Banerjhee reflected, she pretty much was. Clearly. "Like that butterfly on my asscheek?" she smiled over her shoulder, as she skipped away.

Banerjhee smiled and shook his head. "Who wouldn't?"

On the television to his left a tape or program started, consisting of highlights from certain events occurring in Manhattan on September 11, 2001. This made Banerjhee very uneasy.

Toby, meanwhile, had found his cellphone which, despite the gloom, was obviously red and blue with white stars all over it. A patriotic cellphone. He answered it and not ten seconds passed before he said, "Listen, asshole, I told you to call once, and only once. Which part of that don't you understand? No," he shook his head. "Everybody gets treated the same way." He rolled his eyes. "I don't give a fuck." He listened. "I still don't give a fuck." He paced the room. "Now I really don't give a fuck." He shook his head. "I'll call you when I'm ready to call you." He listened. "That makes two of us." He closed the phone and laid it on top of the right-hand television. On its screen a man was patting the hood of an automobile foremost in a long row of them. An American flag flapped from every car antenna in the shot.

Banerjhee glanced away from that screen only to discover that, on the other screen, naked people were having sex.

Toby joined him on the couch.

Banerjhee had never found himself in a social situation quite like this one. He hardly knew what to say. As a result, adding to his discomfort, for a few minutes he and Toby viewed pornography together.

From the kitchen came the unmistakable sound of ice in a cocktail shaker. Well, Banerjhee reflected, maybe Esme does know how to make a martini. Who would have thought that Toby Pride owned a cocktail shaker?

"Now stick it to her," Toby abruptly said, throwing a fist toward the floor.

A man on the screen appeared to oblige him.

"So, umm," Banerjhee said, unwilling to sit there all night watching pornography, "what else is on?"

"Come on, man, quit your—what?" Toby interrupted his concentration to glance at Banerjhee.

"What . . . uh, happened to that World Trade Center footage?"

"Oh," Toby said, "you can't get away from that shit. Haven't you noticed it?"

Rather than nonplusing this budding acquaintance by flatly declaring his strict abjuration of the medium, Banerjhee simply said, "No. I haven't noticed it."

"Some guy in the neighborhood spends all his time jamming this one porn channel."

"Do you spend all your time watching it?" Banerjhee asked him frankly.

Toby lit a cigarette. This startled Banerjhee, who hadn't seen a cigarette smoked indoors in many years. "I called the damn cable company about it." Toby exhaled smoke, and Banerjhee found himself wondering whether or not it might be too cold in Chicago to force people to smoke outside.

"Haven't you noticed that weird truck?" Toby asked. "Dragging the neighborhood at all hours of the day and night? It's a HumVee, for chrissakes, and not just any HumVee; it's the big military model. You can't miss it."

Banerjhee had missed it.

"Well," Toby continued, "it's flat black from bumper to bumper, with antennas all over the roof, tinted windows all round, and bulletproof tires for all I know. I can't believe you haven't seen it." He shook his head. "It's the cable company's stalking vehicle."

"Now that you describe it, I can't believe I haven't noticed it either. But I haven't. How is this guy jamming your signal? And why?"

Toby blew a smoke ring at the screen. "I asked them that. Apparently he taps the output of a small radio receiver into a cable repeater module. These modules are all over the place—on poles, in ground boxes, on the sides of buildings—and they're not hard to break into. I'm not clear on the technicalities but the cable techs tell me that if they find and disable a receiver, within a few days there's a new one in operation. The receivers are homemade and nicely done, apparently. Neatly wired, well-soldered, with untraceable generic parts. From a legal point of view the cable company needs to catch him in the act of vandalizing or broadcasting or both, neither of which they've managed to do. Meanwhile their truck can make a fella a little paranoid, you know? This pirate broadcaster, on the other hand, seems to know when their truck is coming around, because when it does, his signal is nowhere to be found. Here he is again."

Grainy footage of an airplane striking a World Trade Center

building flickered on the screen, backed by strains of the national anthem.

"Sometimes he'll read or recite or improvise these diatribes. They're never quite the same and they always seem to be broadcast live, but they always say the same things, about how America deserved this shit from Osama bin Laden because we allowed him and his culture to flourish, we should have wiped out Islam in the Crusades, and on and on, ad—ad. . . ." The coal of Toby's cigarette hand made circles in the gloom.

"Ad nauseam?"

"That's it—what you said. It's not too coherent, either. He's a confused dude who can't quite get his story straight."

"So why do you watch?"

"Hell," Toby enthused around the speckled filter, clenched between his teeth. "When they catch him, maybe there'll be a big shootout, you know? Hate to miss it." He plucked the cigarette from his teeth and pointed it. "That's why I'm taping it 24/7, in case I'm not here when it happens. This other rig," he pointed at the right-hand set, "will catch the feeds from news choppers when they go live with the story. There's a second VCR for that."

In the shadows beyond the second screen, toward the bottom of the tower of stereo equipment, a red light glowed adjacent a pale blue LCD on which digits ticked.

"He scrambles his voice, too," Toby continued. He slapped Banerjhee's knee and grinned. "Until tonight, me and Esme, we thought it was you."

"What?" Banerjhee retorted, startled. "Me?"

"Yeah, sure." Toby carved the ash off the cigarette with the tip of his ring finger. "Unemployed, smart, degrees in science, time on your hands, maybe some resentment—why not?"

"You forgot brown skin," Banerjhee added coldly.

65

"No I didn't," Toby replied with a disarming smile. "And I'll bet the profilers didn't either. And why not?"

"And—a-and why not?" Banerjhee sputtered, "Because I'm an upstanding goshdarned taxpayer, that's why not."

"You know," said Toby, "I did leave that part out. But hey." He slapped Banerjhee's knee. "It ain't you, is it. You're right here. And that guy," he hooked a thumb at the left-hand television, "is right there. Whoever he is."

"Correct," Banerjhee said stiffly, half-suspecting that Toby had been putting him on. "So, really, that's why you watch this trash?"

"Are you kidding? Man, they're gonna call down a SWAT team on this guy when they find him. After all, he's fucking with some cable company's franchise. That's a federal offense. And when it does go down, it's all gonna be broadcast live, just you watch." He pointed the cigarette at the left-hand monitor. "We'll have him on the inside, describing the incoming, yelling propaganda, bargaining for sandwiches, maybe shooting live ammo out the window. And on this other unit we'll have choppers and commentators, rooftop snipers, and a foxy spokeswoman for the cops. You wait." He puffed on his cigarette. "It's gonna be amazing, BJ. Live as it gets. Marshall McLuhan down the rabbit hole. I'll come get you when it happens. Hey, Esme!"

Live as it gets, Banerjhee repeated to himself.

"What," came the reply from the kitchen.

"Bring us a Ranier, Sweetie?"

"Coming up."

"Hey!" Toby snapped his fingers. "You wanna see it?"

"Is there something I haven't already seen?" Banerjhee replied, politely appalled.

Toby stood up. "What? Oh!" He hefted his balls with his cigarette hand. "Yeah," he chuckled, "the winnings. They're still intact."

"From the lottery? You cashed it in already?"

"Already? BJ, man, I was on that payoff like a dog on a drumstick. Took the check straight to the bank and cashed it. I'll show you. It's way cool."

From a half-open drawer in the stereo stack Toby retrieved a dinner plate. He hooked a coffee table beyond the stack with the toe of a boot, dragged it along the carpet to Banerjhee, and placed the plate on the table. On it were four bank-wrapped stacks of hundred dollar bills and a sheaf of loose ones with a rubber band doubled around it. A small, circular makeup mirror was on the table, too, streaked with white dust.

"Check it out," Toby encouraged him. "There's a hundred C-notes in each bank bundle, fifty in the other one. "Ain't it pretty?"

Each paper wrapper was printed with the figure $10,000. Despite that he had never seen such a thing before, Banerjhee looked but did not touch.

Esme glided into the room bearing a tray loaded with two brimming martinis, one tall frosted glass, and a bottle of beer. She moved aside Toby's lottery prize and set the tray on the table. "Voilá. . . ."

"Beautiful," Banerjhee said.

"Yeah," Toby said ruefully.

"Didn't spill a drop, Mr. Banerjhee," Esme said, gingerly handing him his drink. "I haven't lost my touch."

"Cheers," said Banerjhee, raising the glass, which was ice cold.

Esme took up the other martini and touched its base to the rim of Banerjhee's glass. "Long life."

"You can't impress him with that, Esme," Toby grinned. He touched the neck of the green bottle to her glass and to Banerjhee's. "He's already had a long life." He poured beer from bottle to glass, raising both in the uncertain light.

"That's true," said Esme thoughtfully. "But you probably believe in reincarnation?"

"Not at all," Banerjhee said.

A squalling, obviously scrambled voice burst from the compromised cablecast. "Death to America!"

"Come on, dude," Toby snarled at the television. "Live and let live."

"Hey," said Esme, looking from the left-hand television to Banerjhee to Toby. "It's not him."

"The dude is cool," Toby confirmed. He smiled with an air of omniscient munificence at his glass, over the mouth of which foam was forming a perfect white crown atop the beer, rounding above the rim without breaking over it. "How about we drink to being, like, totally unemployed?"

SEVEN

A dventurism will be met with fire," declared the scrambled narrator. Grainy video depicted scenes of dismayed stock-brokers holding their heads on the trading floor of the New York Stock Exchange. Pornography was superimposed on the stock market scenes, or vice versa. They faded in and out of each other.

"This guy's really asking for it," said Toby, dropping the fag end of his cigarette into the empty Ranier bottle. "Does he really expect to equate the stock market with pornography and get away with it?"

"He wouldn't be the first to have drawn the comparison," Banerjhee observed. But what he was really thinking was that people who never watch television leave themselves wide open to the possibility of being struck dumb whenever they're exposed to it.

Toby said simply, "This is unpatriotic. There's gonna be more people after him than mere pissed-off cable television technicians."

"Waging war on false pretenses," Banerjhee replied, after another pause, "is unpatriotic, too."

Toby's head came slowly around on his shoulders. Sidelit by two televisions he somewhat resembled a monitor lizard, lazily checking out the latest tourist to step ashore. "It's unpatriotic to disparage capitalism, BJ," he said simply. "Unpatriotic is ill-advised."

Banerjhee slightly changed the subject. "Do you know anything more about the anti-patriot's technology?"

"It's simple and clever. Basically he uses hotrodded walky-talky technology–that's what the cable tech told me, anyway. They found a receiver in a curb box at Redwood Avenue and Luther Burbank Lane, which is, what, about a mile and a half from here? They reverse-engineered it and figured out his transmitter has a range of no more than three or four miles, so they're canvassing the neighborhood. They didn't knock on your door?"

"No," said Banerjhee thoughtfully.

"Hm," Toby said, perhaps equally thoughtfully. "That's odd."

"I could get paranoid about it," Banerjhee confirmed.

"So could I," Toby agreed.

"You go first."

"All right," Toby said. "First thought, best thought: since you are not white, possess technological ability, and seem to espouse certain liberal opinions, you are suspect."

"Bingo."

"Citizenship means nothing."

"Apparently not."

"No more than a veteran's status."

"I wouldn't know."

Toby frowned. "Where were you during Vietnam? Isn't that about. . . ."

"My era?"

"Yeah. Your era."

"I received a deferment based upon a non-service-related contribution to the war effort."

"Your daddy was governor of Texas?"

70

Banerjhee shook his head.

Toby shrugged. "I just mentioned it because, if he was, that would be pretty patriotic."

"That's not what he—nor I—was doing."

Toby pointed a finger at him. "You worked as a corpsman? In a hospital maybe?"

"I shouldn't talk about it."

"Another martini?"

Banerjhee blinked at his glass. It was empty. "Sure."

"Esme!" Toby raised his voice. "Table service!"

Esme reappeared and looked at the glass. "Don't you want the olive?"

"Oh. Of course." Banerjhee stripped it off the toothpick with his teeth.

"Good?"

"Most tasty." Banerjhee dropped the toothpick into the empty glass and belched politely into his hand.

"See?" she said to Toby. "A gentleman."

Toby affected a bemused expression that made him look entirely capable of belching without using his hand.

Esme turned toward the kitchen and turned back. "I forgot to tell you, Mr. Banerjhee, these olives are garnished with a sliver of habanero. You know your peppers? Is it too hot?"

Banerjhee smacked his lips. "I wondered why it tasted so excellent."

"It's pretty hot," she assured him.

"I must get you to sample my dear wife's chicken *mole* with green chili sauce." The habanero made his eyes tear, and he smiled. "It guarantees good circulation of the blood."

"Why is that?" Esme asked.

"The fourth element is fire. Delivered via cayenne and African bird powder and all kinds of chili peppers, fire helps circulate the blood."

"Fire," squealed the scrambled audio. "Rain of fire!"

71

"Rain or reign?" Toby asked the television.

"Oh," said Esme, "I believe in that. And I'm not even a Scorpio."

"Look at me," Banerjhee chuckled. "I'm a perfect example." He smoothed his pineapple shirt over his modest belly. "Without spicy food, I'd be toast."

Esme giggled and held up the glass. "The same?"

Banerjhee held up two fingers. "May I have two olives, please?"

"Manners. See?" She headed for the kitchen. "Coming right up."

"Now here's a sick fuck," Toby declared.

The left-hand video showed a man wearing a kaftan and pokol, seated outdoors on a rug. An AK-47 assault rifle leaned against a rock in the background. Spanish subtitles crawled across the top of the screen, and English ones crawled across the bottom of it. "Since you don't watch television, I should tell you that's Osama bin Laden, the guy who's credited with masterminding the attacks on the World Trade Center."

"Um," Banerjhee said.

"That's all the attacks mind you, including the one by those idiots from Egypt via the blind mullah from New Jersey who tried to blow up its foundations with a fertilizer bomb in 1993, plus I think a couple of thwarted attempts the government probably hasn't told us about, culminating in the attempt that succeeded in 2001."

"Even I, who merely read the newspapers, know who this guy is," Banerjhee pointed out. "Or was."

Toby turned to look at him. "You know, practically the first time I met you, you mentioned that you don't watch television. Are you hung up or something?"

"I don't even own one. That makes it easy."

"But," Toby said, bemused, "look what you're missing."

Banerjhee looked. On the left-hand monitor rolled the tape

of bin Laden, its original graininess redoubled by the pirate broadcast, superimposed on an orgy scene. On the right-hand monitor a clean cut, slim young man was addressing a couch full of mugging, bright-eyed, acting-school chums. Even with the sound off, or especially with the sound off, one could see each waiting for their cue, following the scripted dialogue with their eyes or delighting in an improvised bit. All the actors were comely, all but one was Caucasian, all wore tailored, pastel clothing. The café set was generic enough to belie any known extant location, as were the perfectly groomed patrons criss-crossing the background. The laws that governed this and nearly every other segment of the televised universe, including Hollywood movies, had nothing to do with the ones that Banerjhee found applicable to his own. He set about telling Toby as much, but before long Toby was laughing. "I know that, BJ, man," he protested. "But the fact is, more and more people find it easier to act like the actors they see on television than to maintain a real-world personality."

"Is that why you watch it?"

"Are you kidding?" Toby said, gesturing at both monitors. "How can you not watch? It's the trainwreck of everything!"

"Toby, my friend," Banerjhee said, after a moment's reflection, "I believe you have perfectly expressed the contrapositive of the reason that I don't watch."

"What did you say?"

"If television is the trainwreck of everything," Banerjhee said, extending his own hand toward the two monitors, "then Not-television is the Not-trainwreck of everything."

While Banerjhee's logic, if only half-joking, had not necessarily stumped Toby, Toby wasn't going to concede the point. To play for time, or because he was addicted to nicotine, Toby lit another cigarette. "But, BJ, there's really lots of good stuff on television." He blew smoke at the right-hand screen and waved his hand through the plume. "I don't mean this bullshit. I mean like the History Channel." He turned to look at Banerjhee. "There's lots of good stuff on the Nature Channel, too. It can be very educational." Toby parked the cigarette on the corner of his lower lip and scratched his still-naked thigh with the freed-up hand. The other held a remote control loosely but surely, in much the same way a cowboy holds a coiled riata and watches his milling livestock. "And don't forget them bicycle races, live from Europe in the middle of the night."

"I'll bet they're just perfect for insomnia," Banerjhee nodded. "Plus, I suspect the Nature Channel saves a lot of people the trouble of going places about which they otherwise might remain curious, thus sparing them expense and mosquito bites and whatnot. In turn the pertinent wildlife and wilderness are excused from the directly proportionate abuse of tourism, a result one can only condone."

Toby shook his head. "Man," he laughed, "you are an un-forgiving, judgmental asshole." He looked at Banerjhee in dead earnest. "Most people are just doing the best they can."

Banerjhee smiled affably. "Are you trying to depress me?"

Toby clucked his tongue. "Shit. I got pills for that."

Esme returned to present another martini, droplets of condensation runneling its frosty cone. Two olives on a toothpick bobbed gently in the icy vodka like a man over-board buoy in a slack Arctic tide. Banerjhee ate one immediately.

On the left-hand screen the speech was now replaced by almost incomprehensible green and black night-vision images of smart bombs, missiles, rockets, tracer bullets and other ordnance raining down on Baghdad in 1993.

"There," Toby pointed his cigarette. "My war."

A logo in the lower left-hand corner of the screen identified the footage as having been broadcast by CNN. An Arabic voice-over, barely perceptible behind the explosions, faded in and out of pornographic grunts.

"But still," Banerjhee began, taking a sip of his martini. "Most excellent," he said to Esme, who smiled with pleasure.

"The sick fuck," Toby muttered.

Banerjhee pointed a toothpicked olive at the left-hand screen, which had cut back to the bin Laden tape with its two sets of subtitles. "What makes him sick?"

"Oh," Toby said, "not him. He's just an asshole. I'm talking about whoever's doing the broadcasting. He's screwing up the only porn channel you can get with this subscription."

"How many channels come with the subscription?"

"Two-fifty-something?"

"Two thirty-five," Esme emended, seating herself in a rattan easy chair immediately to Banerjhee's left.

"All that and only one porn channel?"

Toby shrugged. "It's all pornographic."

"Maybe the company's owned by Christians," Esme suggested. "You want another greenie?"

"Yeah." Toby dropped the stub of his second cigarette into the mouth of the first empty, saying to Banerjhee, "But happily, you ain't him."

"Well, that's a relief," Banerjhee admitted. He couldn't imagine spending any time at all thinking about video tape, let alone watching enough television to archive stock sufficient to keep the likes of Toby amused. If Toby were paying attention, he might have already come to that conclusion about Banerjhee. In any case, it seemed a reasonable mercy to have been stricken from the list of suspects.

More bombing footage. Scrambled chicken-clucking cluttered the audio.

"So now," Toby said, scratching his unkempt hair, "tell us again what you did during the war?"

"I never told you in the first place."

Toby spread his arms. "What the fuck possible difference could it make at this point?" He gestured at the televisions. "We're four or five wars down the road, here."

Banerjhee considered it. "I'll tell you this much," he decided, "My contribution involved chemical engineering. The project never amounted to anything, and so it was never deployed. I spent only five months on the project before it was scrapped, after which I was excused from further service."

"So it was like a Star Wars kind of thing?"

Banerjhee frowned, had a sip of martini, and considered. "Far-fetched, you mean? The last time I checked, the so-called Star Wars weapons program involved politicians telling physicists that it ain't no hill for high-stepping American know-how to convoke near-instantaneous three-bank snooker shots in the ionosphere—does that fairly describe Star Wars?"

"Beats me," Toby frankly admitted.

"I thought it had something to do with national security," Esme volunteered from the kitchen doorway.

"Leaving that aside," Banerjhee nodded, "it describes Star Wars for me, and I'm the only scientist in the room. Correct?"

"Except for the mixologist," Toby pointed out, as Esme handed him a beer.

"Far-fetched, then. It's not uncommon. To reinforce the point, I'll sketch what I did for the war effort of my . . . era. The Vietnam War." Banerjhee gestured toward both monitors. "The first televised war, among other things."

"The first war America ever lost," Esme noted.

"Hey," said Toby.

"Among many other things," Banerjhee amended.

"A story." Esme sat on the rattan chair and crossed her legs. "I'm all ears."

"Baby," said Toby, as if poaching the thought from Banerjhee's mind, "You're a lot more than ears."

"One fine day," Banerjhee began, "I was sitting around my

place in Menlo Park, trying to write a Basic program that would sort free radicals by ordinal number."

Esme's face remained frozen in pleasure. "What did you say?"

"Well, since you asked, oxidation reactions leave you with organic compounds; under certain conditions, some valence electrons remain unpaired." Banerjhee waved a hand. "But skip it."

Everybody had a sip of a drink. Esme asked seriously, "Isn't rust an oxidation process?"

"Yes it is, Esmerelda, and so is fire."

"You mean," Esme said, "when you bite into a habanero pepper, your tongue is being oxidized?"

"Hmm. I was referring to actual flames—paper or wood or anything, burning in the presence of oxygen. But you know, Esme, yours is an interesting premise." Banerjhee took a sip of martini. "I shall undertake some pepper research and get back to you."

"Oh." Esme waved a hand in embarrassment. "Don't go to all that trouble."

"No trouble at all. A pleasure. Who knows? We might learn something."

"Maybe you could do a special on the Food Network," Toby suggested.

"That," Banerjhee said with certainty, "I do not have the time to undertake."

"So oxidation," Esme reminded him.

"Yes. Well, it was in the early days of computing, very early, but that's not even the point. There came a knock at the door."

"Uh-oh," Toby said, wiping his chin with his forearm.

"In so many words," Banerjhee agreed. "Two men introduced themselves, one as a civilian contractor who worked for the Department of Defense, and the other, so far as I could tell, pretty much *was* the Department of Defense. This latter character showed me a draft notice—my draft notice—then he folded it into a stamped envelope which was addressed to me. Accept my colleague's suggestions re a rare opportunity to render great service to your country, he explained, or this envelope goes into the nearest mailbox."

"Just like that?" Toby said. "No tests, no physical, no nothing? What about your college deferment?"

Banerjhee shook his head. "Just like that."

"Persuasive," Esme observed.

"Long story short," Banerjhee nodded grimly, "I found myself in the desert, southeast of Salt Lake City, living and working in an underground laboratory populated entirely by co-workers of whom I was allowed to discover little more than first names along with inklings of their specializations."

"Isn't that," Esme said slowly, "not very far from where some kind of government experiment with anthrax went haywire and killed eight or ten thousand sheep?"

"Not very far at all," Banerjhee confirmed quietly.

"What in the world were you doing there, Mr. Banerjhee?" Esme tucked one heel under a thigh and steadied her martini on the calf.

"Okay," Toby interrupted. "Now you just about have to tell us what the hell you were doing."

"No, I don't. I can't. I can't tell you the specifics of the work," Banerjhee replied seriously. "I signed an oath of secrecy. The details wouldn't mean anything to you anyway. Suffice to say, my work involved organic chemistry."

"You were making poison gas?" Esme asked, appalled.

"No," Banerjhee replied forcefully. "Not poison gas."

"Thank god," Esme said sincerely.

"But why you?" Toby frowned. "No offense, but at any given moment, California must be full of people who can do organic chemistry. I mean, full professors of organic chemistry. Guys who wrote the books."

"True enough. And I can explain that part because it isn't secret, which will clue you in to what we were doing, but you didn't hear it from me." Banerjhee looked at each of them and each shrugged.

"Sure," Esme said.

"Fair enough," Toby said.

"I'm afraid it's equal parts incredible and insidious."

"Groovy."

"Why?"

"What those two government guys knew about me was that I had spent an undergraduate summer in Basel–that's in Switzerland–as a lab assistant in a certain pharmaceutical firm."

Toby frowned. "Why does that ring a bell?

Esme shook her head, puzzled. "Should it?"

"Well, well," Banerjhee marveled. "Time is a marvelous thing. Right here in California, too."

"Sure we have time in California," Esme said. "Don't they have it everywhere?"

"I suppose they do," Banerjhee said, bemused.

"So what's the big deal about a student summer in the Alps?" she asked.

"Well, there was a very great chemist there, in whose work our government, not to mention quite a number of other people, had taken a strong interest. The first thing that shook me up was that those two government guys knew I had worked specifically under him. The records weren't secret or anything, and I was naive, but how the hell did they know to seek me out?"

"You're still being naive," Toby confirmed.

"I suppose so. Within a few days of the interview I had a draft deferment, a ticket to Salt Lake City, and a two-year sabbatical from Stanford."

"What was this chemist's name?" Toby asked.

79

"More to the point, what was he up to that was so all-fired interesting?" Esme asked.

Banerjhee said nothing.

Toby snapped a finger and pointed it at Banerjhee. "Chemical warfare, with a twist. You were making acid gas. Battlefield acid gas. Weaponized LSD. Or psilocybin? Maybe mescaline."

"Did I say that?" Banerjhee asked.

"Really?" Esme said, aghast.

"You'd make a good detective." Banerjhee said to Toby.

"No I wouldn't," Toby replied, not missing a beat. "I like being loaded too much."

"I'll bet you were good at it, too," Esme said admiringly.

Banerjhee took the next-to-last sip from his martini. "You didn't hear it from me."

"Shit," Toby said, "what a bunch of idiots. You turn acid gas loose on a battlefield and everybody would go crazy. They'd lay down their guns or shoot themselves or shoot each other. What was the brass thinking? There'd be no way to control it."

"So they concluded—eventually." Banerjhee held his martini with both hands and watched it with a strange expression on his face. "It took an accident to convince them, however."

"An accident. You mean—like with the sheep?"

"Yes," Banerjhee said thoughtfully. "Except nobody died."

"I bet somebody thought he died," Toby remarked.

"The entire facility was air-conditioned," Banerjhee said simply, "and it was completely underground. There was only one way in or out, which was a long, brightly lit concrete ramp. Security personnel had to open a pair of big motorized steel doors at the upper end first, though, before anybody could come or go. The doors were blast-proof and it was probably fifteen years before I saw another digital lock even remotely comparable." Banerjhee stared shyly into his martini. His eyes shone and a little smile played over his lips. "For a while there, nobody could remember the combination."

Toby and Esme exchanged an astonished glance.

"It was bound to happen," Banerjhee said, "sooner or later." He nodded at the memory. "Sooner was better."

After a long pause Esme looked from Banerjhee to Toby and back. "Is that it?"

"I've never told this to anyone before." Banerjhee looked up and added quietly, "Not even to Madja." He looked down at his drink again.

After perhaps a full minute of solemn silence, Toby cleared his throat and said, "That's some of the craziest shit I ever heard."

Esme nodded, then shook her head, wordlessly.

Banerjhee finished his drink, set the glass on the tray, and stripped the remaining olive off its toothpick with his teeth. "I was very glad to get back to California," he said, chewing.

EIGHT

Goddamn thing," Toby said, without explanation. He pulled at his right cowboy boot. "Like to carve a hole in my ankle bone." The boot abruptly came off, and a derringer fell to the carpet with a thump.

"Is that a pistol?" Banerjhee asked, somewhat lamely.

"Sure," said Toby, inspecting his exposed ankle. "It's a derringer. Honey, I need a bandage."

"In the bathroom."

Toby limped into the gloom beyond the stereo stack.

"A double-barreled derringer," Banerjhee said, looking without touching.

"Stupid," Esme said.

"It looks like a cigarette lighter," Banerjhee said, studying it.

"It'll light more than cigarettes." Toby reappeared and paused in front of the right-hand television to strip the packaging off a square adhesive bandage.

"You should wear a sock," Esme suggested.

"Too crowded." Toby propped his foot atop the television and applied the bandage to the outside shank of his leg, just above the point of his ankle.

Banerjhee pointed at the empty boot on the floor. "What's it doing . . . in there?"

Toby's dropped his foot to the floor and moved both hands

up and down as if to outline his naked torso. "Where the fuck else would I keep it?"

"Up your ass," Esme suggested cheerfully, gesturing with her martini. "Right next to your brain."

Banerjhee giggled.

"It needs to be where somebody besides you can get at it," Toby responded. "Me, for instance. And when the time comes, you'll be glad."

"Toby," Esme preened, "you're all man. One hundred percent bona fido dumb-ass Homo sapiens."

"Woof."

"Good dog." They both giggled. It was a different giggle than the one Banerjhee had giggled: less nervous.

Banerjhee gestured toward the pistol. "May I. . . ?"

"Why sure," Toby said, plucking up the tiny weapon and unceremoniously dropping it into Banerjhee's lap. "Check it out. She's the genuine article. A real conversation piece." He winked. "Like Esme, there."

"One of these days," Esme assured him, "I'm going to talk your head off."

"Careful," Toby cautioned. He covered the pistol with his hand. "It's loaded."

"And the next day," Esme continued, "that toy's gonna blow your foot off."

"It's not a toy and I don't doubt it," Toby assured her. "But if we don't have sex soon, this bickering is going to turn nasty."

"If you're going to get anywhere with me," Esme put her nose into the air, "you're going to have to address the subject in a more allegorical manner."

"Ahm," Toby fretted, "Please?"

"No."

"Pretty please?"

"Nope."

"How about, give it to me, you—"

"Is it really loaded?" Banerjhee interrupted, not touching the pistol.

Toby retrieved the gun, broke it down, and inverted it over the startled Banerjhee's hand. "Not any more." He snapped the breach closed and laughed.

The brass firing caps on the bullets looked the size of dimes, **.357 MAG** embossed in an arc on each.

Toby reversed the pistol in his hand, holding it by the barrel. "See that handle? What do you think? It's about the size and color of a shucked oyster? Yes? No?"

Indeed the nacre handle was very small, with a slight curve to it, slim and not much more than two inches long, very smooth. The trigger didn't have a guard on it, which may have explained the irritation inside Toby's boot.

"Is it chrome?"

"Stainless steel."

"There are two barrels but one trigger," Banerjhee noticed.

"Progressive firing pin," Toby explained. "You see that with over-and-unders. Take it away from me."

Banerjhee tentatively pinched the tiny pistol grip. Leaving his trigger finger for the trigger, he could only get a thumb on one side of the grip and two fingers on the other side.

"Them two fingers reach so far along the chambers they get powder burns," Toby told him. "Now pull." Banerjhee pulled and his fingers slipped off the grip. "See?" Banerjhee tried again. Toby laughed and let him take the gun. "It's a belly gun, no doubt about it." He retrieved the two slugs and the pistol, re-loaded it and snapped the breech shut. "Which is just as well, because if you don't hold it against the target. . . ." He poked the short twin barrel into Banerjhee's ribs and grinned.

"Toby," Esme objected, "you're being stupid."

Toby's face was not ten inches from Banerjhee's, and its vanguard of beer breath enveloped him. "That little grip is so small, and this," he screwed the barrels into Banerjhee's shirt, "is so much pistol that—when you pull the trigger? Boom!" Banerjhee jumped. Pride laughed. "You get a big hole on one end and a missing pistol on the other. You can't hold onto it." Pride laughed louder and threw up his hands. "The goddamn thing disappears!"

Banerjhee blinked and nodded, as if in agreement with everything Toby was saying.

To Banerjhee's left, Esme sat with her back straight and her legs crossed as if she were chatting at a cocktail party. "One time, when Toby was trying to learn how to shoot that thing? What he really learned was that one shot is all you get. One shot. Then you have to go hunting for the lil' sucker."

"The first time we shot it I wasn't paying too much attention," Toby admitted. "Probably the tequila."

"Or the beer," Esme pointed out.

"Or the oxycodone. Whatever."

Esme made a face at Banerjhee as if to say, Can you believe this guy? Isn't he cute?

"I hit the fence I was aiming at," Toby continued, "which was a good thing because it was only ten feet away. But we spent the next hour combing through the brush where I'd been standing when I pulled the trigger, looking for the damn gun."

"It shoots pretty straight, actually." Esme squinted along her cocked forefinger. "You have to make sure whoever is with you stands well behind you. Because when it goes off—poof!" She threw up her hands. "No way you can hang on to it! It could sock a bystander in the head!"

When their laughter subsided Toby said, "We finally broadened the search and found it about six feet up a manzanita tree, propped in a fork."

"It looked like somebody deliberately left it there," Esme said.

Toby sat down next to Banerjhee and pulled on his boot. "It's a little inconvenient, but it's hard to find a gun this small with stopping power. You talk about punch?" Toby nodded sagely. "Knock down any man, any time." He delicately slid the pistol into the boot cuff.

"It sounds like it might knock down the man who's firing it, too," Banerjhee said.

"Only if he manages to hold onto it," Toby reassured him, which set him and Esme to laughing again.

"It's somewhat of a novelty piece," Esme admitted.

"Better than nothing," Toby said, sipping his beer. He stood up and moved the green bottle around his profile as if it were a hand-held metal detector. "And nothing is just about what I got on."

Banerjhee didn't ask him why he didn't put on some clothes. Toby was in his own home, after all.

"What do you think, Mr. Banerjhee." Esme resettled into the chair with her ankles tucked beneath her thighs. "Not a bad physique for a guy who lives on beer and pizza, huh?"

"Screeenova," squawked the scrambled voice from the left-hand television. "Readin the government email."

"Hey," said Toby. "This is a daily feature."

The voice sounded like a ghoul in a cheap horror film. The electronic box that makes this effect, Banerjhee reflected, must be readily available at your better guitar stores.

"To the President of the United States," declaimed the voice. "Your foreign and domestic policies are like continual drops of water in the face of the body politic."

"I'm going to have to think about that one," said Esme.

"Me, too," said Banerjhee.

"Shh," Toby hushed them

Skroiuuunt–"Why have we had no discussion of the Euro becoming the new global standard of exchange for OPEC, thereby usurping the preeminence of the US Dollar? My

87

listeners, people of the so-called Free World, put this question in email to your congressman. Email your president at WWW dot whitehouse dot gov and demand an explanation. Email God, who mulls various applications of His terrible wrath."

"He doesn't seem to have much of an accent," Esme observed.

"He does have a certain slant," Banerjhee pointed out.

"He does at that," she agreed.

"He sounds like a Saturday morning cartoon," Toby said.

On the screen, jets flew over the camera from behind the point of view and into the far distance of the frame. Explosions followed. The frame shook. "Today in Hebron," a normal television newscaster's voice declared, "Israeli military jets pounded Palestinian terrorist positions."

"You know," said the scrambled voice, "just once in a while— once in a while!—they should reverse the two adjectives."

"How's that?" Banerjhee asked aloud.

"Israeli terrorist jets," the voice replied, "pounded Palestinian military positions. Skroieuuuinch!"

"He heard you," Esme said without conviction.

Toby's cell phone began to recite God Bless America. "Now what?"

Banerjhee shrugged. "To some he's got a point, of that I am certain. Not to everybody, however."

"Well duh," Esme admonished. "Have you never watched an Arab television channel?"

"Never," Banerjhee said.

"But you don't watch this shit, either," Esme said, before Banerjhee could say it.

"True."

"I guess that makes you even."

"Or something," Banerjhee agreed with a sigh.

Now hundreds if not thousands of people screamed and waved banners at the screen. "Thousands of years," bayed the scrambled voice. "Why should they stop now? Give them a reason! Give them a reason! Give them a reason!"

The picture abruptly displayed three naked men having sex with one naked woman. After a moment Banerjhee said, "It looks like a motel room."

"When the Israeli army takes over Palestinian television, as they do periodically," the scrambled voice said, "this is what they broadcast to God's people. Twenty-four seven. This filth!"

"You think these people do this stuff at home?" Banerjhee idly asked.

"I think motel rooms turn them on," Esme replied, "and they don't have to clean up afterward."

Superimposed over the pornography was a slow pan of naked children with swollen bellies, looking with big eyes into the camera, their legs emaciated by rickets, the image ghosting in and out of the motel four-way. The scrambled voice returned. "Around the world, children are starving. Around the world, every year, AIDS kills millions. Around the world, a few profiteers smuggle munitions to bloodthirsty insurgencies. International aid is stolen and traded for arms. Weapons whose destructive power is almost beyond belief fall into the hands of—*skrak!*"

The voice and images ceased. After a moment of snow and hiss, the audio of the pornography—a steady throb of a single synthesizer with grunting and breathing—resumed. After another moment the entire screen filled with human genitalia.

"Toby," Esme said. "Something seems to be happening with Scramble Man."

Toby rematerialized out of the far shadows of the living room, whence he had retired to talk. With the phone clenched between his shoulder and ear, he regarded the screen of the right-hand television, then bent to push a button, causing the unit to scan through a handful of pre-selected channels.

89

Talking head after talking head appeared, all of them looking alike and doing more or less the same thing. One spoke of the crash of a passenger jet in Namibia. Another discussed the weather. A third was onto the unfortunate score of a football game. A fourth quoted from a statement issued by the vice-President.

"These are all the local news outlets," Esme explained to Banerjhee. "Is the tape running?"

Toby glanced toward the tape machine at the bottom of the stereo stack and grunted. Abruptly he said into the phone, "Listen, Carlos, I told you, it's not set up yet. It's weird over here; we shouldn't even be discussing it." He listened for a moment. "Sure it's an encoded call," he said impatiently. "But–" He listened. "But you don't understand, there's a scene going on over here, there's some nut jamming the local TV signals. You should see the truck the FCC or whoever's got roaming the streets. It looks like something out of *War Between The Worlds*. What? Uh . . . *Guerra Dentro Los Mundos.*" He shook his head. "Skip it. The fucking point was, who knows how many other cruisers they–"

Toby spun on the heels of his cowboy boots, caught Esme's eye, and raised his free hand in an open gesture, as in, what can I do? Then he paced back into the darkness beyond the stereo equipment.

"That Toby," Esme said admiringly. "He could talk a groupie out of her backstage pass."

"Why would he want to do that?" Banerjhee asked.

Esme laughed. "The only thing that really bugs me about him is he smokes. Otherwise he's a perfect specimen."

"He should quit," Banerjhee agreed pedantically. "Something like 60% of all cancers are in one way or another attributable to cigarette smoking."

"So I've told him. His snappy comeback is something else will kill him first."

Toby returned from the shadows. Making as if to slam his cellphone down onto the top of the right-hand television, he pulled the blow at the last moment, and gently traded it for a remote control.

"Sonofabitch?" Esme said, anticipating him.

"Sonofabitch," Toby agreed. "They have the shit, for which we paid only half in front, which they don't usually let people do. We were supposed to come up with the other half the day before yesterday. Now they're nervous."

"Did you explain about the lottery?" Esme asked.

"No," Toby replied, annoyed, "I didn't tell the fucking Colombians about the fucking lottery. They don't like extraneous information."

"Otherwise known as excuses."

"Exactly." He pointed the wand at the left-hand television. "They don't give a shit about the HumVee."

"So?"

Toby pursed his lips and regarded the modest stack of bills on the coffee table. "So it was a mistake to let Chase handle the fina–"

"Anyway," Esme interrupted him, "$45,000 is a little short."

Toby raised an eyebrow.

"Where's Chase?"

Toby shook his head. "LA. He had a trial."

"I thought–" Esme stopped. After thirty seconds she said, "Maybe we should get dressed."

"Listen, BJ, man," Toby said suddenly, but still distracted, not quite bestirring himself from another line of thought, "I think it's time you went home."

Startled, Banerjhee looked from Esme to Toby and back again. "I beg your pardon?"

"It's been a pleasure, Mr. Banerjhee," Esme said. She dropped her feet from the chair cushion to the floor and set her half-finished martini on the coffee table.

"Oh. I. . . . Of course," Banerjhee stammered, without getting up. "I . . . had a wonderful time," he continued without much conviction. "Thank you so . . . much for your hospitality." His eye fell on the glasses on the coffee table. "Do you need help with the dishes?"

Esme smiled at him fondly. "No, Mr. Banerjhee," she said. "I think you've done quite enough for one evening, smoothing our feathers and all. You were quite helpful, in fact. It was kind of you to take the time."

"Oh," Banerjhee said dismissively, "it wasn't anything anybody else wouldn't do."

"I doubt that, Mr. Banerjhee," Esme said, as Banerjhee struggled with the enveloping sofa. "I doubt that very much." She offered her hand. "Let me help you."

Somewhat taken aback by the abrupt withdrawal of their hospitality, Banerjhee now found himself flummoxed by the apparently bottomless cushions and voracious corduroy of the low couch, not to mention the effect of two martinis. He forestalled Esme's offer with his own hand. "Just let me collect myself," he protested. "I don't often take so much to drink. Moreover, it's strange to observe, but it's true, rarely do I become so comfortable in another person's living room."

"Uh huh," Toby replied coldly. "Shake a leg,"

"That's a very kind thing of you to say, Mr. Banerjhee," Esme said, shooting a remonstrative glance at Toby, who rolled his eyes. She pulled Banerjhee up from the couch. "We don't often have such polite company, I'm sure, and we hardly ever get called away on business or whatever. Perhaps you'll come another time."

Having achieved the vertical, Banerjhee glanced at his watch. "Two-thirty in the morning," he said in surprise. "Little wonder I feel so tired." He looked at Toby, who was clearly thinking about something else. He looked at Esme, whose smile appeared strained. "Do you happen to recall where you laid my jacket?"

From the garage door came a loud crash, then a second one, followed by the splintering of wood and the tinkle of broken glass.

"Shit," Esme breathed. "That was quick."

Toby swiftly cut his left arm against the backs of Banerjhee's knees and pushed down on Banerjhee's right shoulder with his right hand, causing Banerjhee to sit abruptly back down on the couch. Toby put his mouth next to Banerjhee's right ear and said quietly, "Keep your head down, BJ," and turned the couch over on top of him.

Empty pizza boxes clattered to the kitchen linoleum, and a beam of light swiveled into the living room.

"Freeze!" a man shouted.

A second male voice added, with a distinctly Spanish accent, "Nobody moves, nobody speaks."

NINE

Freeze is false emphasis, Banerjhee found himself thinking, and misplaced emphasis trivializes. Lying on the floor beneath the upturned couch, he found that the scene in the living room was reflected in the plate glass door looming above him. Two men had crowded into the room. A third stood in the doorway. All were armed and wore black ski masks.

"Stand up, lady," said the man with the Spanish accent.

"Wow," said the second man, behind the first, forgetting to point his gun at Esme. "Nice."

"Shut up," barked the first man. "You with the little dick." He pointed a nasty-looking machine pistol with a banana clip at the ceiling, his trigger finger alongside its trigger guard, and pointed his other trigger finger at the pile of money on the coffee table. "That's a good start. Where's the stash?"

Toby blinked at him, glanced at the second man, then slowly spread his hands. "Search me, dude. I was looking for it myself. It ain't under the couch, as you can see. But hey. . . ." Toby raised his hands elbow high and turned smoothly around until he was facing away from the gunman. "Why don't you search my searchable cavity?" he suggested mildly. He bent forward and loudly passed wind.

Rage bulged the eyes in the first ski mask, and they looked

perfectly capable of ordering a compliant trigger finger to cause Toby's searchable cavity to be filled with lead.

"Here," Toby added, "let me help you." He spread his left ass cheek with his left hand, shifting his weight onto that leg and inserted his right hand into the cuff of his right cowboy boot as he did so. Then he hoisted the boot high into the air behind him and screamed "Asshole!" as he fired the derringer.

The detonation blew off most of the side and heel of the red boot and quite a bit of Toby's instep, too, in a spray of smoke and bone and flesh and shredded leather. Toby let out a roar of pain and amazement—"The cocksucker STILL got away from me!"—and pitched forward onto his face. Even so, the 125-grain .357 Magnum slug caught the first gunman squarely in the larynx with momentum sufficient to knock him backwards, into the arms of the man behind him.

The second man caught the first man and unsentimentally steadied the body in front of him like a shield. He was calmly stitching a line of gore diagonally up the back side of Toby's entire torso, from right calf to left shoulder blade, when Esme shot the man twice in his right ear with a .25 caliber Browning automatic pistol she had slipped from beneath the cushion of the rattan chair as soon as she heard the kitchen door splinter.

The third man put a short burst from his weapon into a tight circle just above Esme's left breast. Five or six copper-jacketed .225 slugs chewed all the way through Esme and punched holes into the sheetrock wall behind her. She crumpled to the floor at the third man's feet but he gave her a second short burst anyway. And he might well have administered a *miserichorde* to her ear had not Banerjhee dropped him like a sack of wet sand with the second shot from the derringer, fired over the upended bottom of the couch at a range of six feet.

Smoke drifted through the TV-lit air of the living room of

the single-story, fifties-style, California ranch home, as the ineluctable silence of suburbia straightened its bib and reconvened its meal of tranquility.

Very tentatively, Banerjhee peered over the couch, behind which he'd ducked as soon as he'd pulled the trigger. The derringer had disappeared and his hand throbbed like he'd closed it in a car door, but he barely noticed.

Squeeeeeeeeeeree-ree-ree. . . . said the left-hand television. "Readin' the government's email."

Everybody was dead.

Skwoi.

Almost everybody.

Banerjhee crawled to the stage-left end of the sofa. Attempting to discern a pulse in the gloom he inadvertently inserted his finger into a bullet hole in Esme's throat. Surely, she had died instantly.

Squoi, said the television. *Flibberty-gibbit.*

He back-crawled behind the sofa to its opposite end, then crawled forward, toward the left-hand television. On the way the heel of his bloodied left hand rolled off a windrow of shell casings. The arm went out from under him and his chin whacked an edge of the coffee table. He sat up and rubbed his jaw. Everything on the coffee table remained quite undisturbed. The plateful of lottery money, the cocaine-dusted compact mirror, two empty martini glasses, a glass and two beer bottles looked as neutral as a prop belonging to some other melodrama.

Shielding his eyes from the pornographic glare he found the volume controls on both televisions and turned them down. He left their pictures on because he wanted the light.

A whisper, barely audible in the silence, so subtle it might have been an anomaly, seemed a distant sound borne on the slightest of breezes.

"BJ. . . ."

If the voice of Kali Destroyer had called him, Banerjhee could not have been more startled. But he was certain it had been real, that it had been there to be heard, and that he had heard it. In the silence that ensued he thought maybe the term freeze not so falsely emphatic after all.

Kali would have called him by his proper name. No? Yes? "Toby?"

In the obscurity he could see the fallen Toby's left hand, practically the only part of the nude body not covered in blood. The back of the wrist lay against the floor. As Banerjhee stared, its fingers curled away from the floor.

"Toby!" He stopped by the second television long enough to angle it toward the back of the room, then crawled to the body. Once there he hesitated. Was it not not good to disturb a recently machine-gunned person? He turned and retrieved Toby's all-American cellphone from the top of the right-hand television, took a deep breath, and forced himself to think. He stammered aloud. "I must call. Nine. One. One. That's it. Nine . . . one and one." He had to recite the numbers aloud to be sure of them. He'd never called the combination before in his life. The cell-phone keypad illuminated as he lifted the lid. He remembered somebody remarking that dialing 9-1-1 on a cellphone might get him any police department on the West Coast. Something to do with placement of transmission towers, or satellite triangulation, or emerging technology. Well, it would have to make for a start. . . .

"BJ," Toby whispered to the rug.

Banerjhee dropped the phone and scuttled back to Toby. He thought it unwise but after some dithering and as gently as possible he turned over the body. There was so much blood it sounded as if he were prying a sheet of plywood out of a mud flat.

Toby's complexion being drained of all color, the flickering palette of the two televisions lent it various hues, all of them ghastly. But Toby smiled weakly at the ceiling. "You made it, man."

Banerjhee touched two fingers to the carotid beneath Toby's jaw. He could barely feel it. There was no mystery about that. Much of the man's blood was on the floor.

"No use," Toby whispered. "Esme?"

Banerjhee glanced her way but said nothing.

"Shit," Toby hissed. "I must. . . ." He closed his eyes.

After a long moment Banerjhee said, "I should. . . ."

Pride's fingers plucked feebly at his. The gesture read like a negative. Hold on, it said, my girlfriend just got gunned down in my own living room. Give me a minute.

After an incalculable unit of time had passed, Banerjhee tried again. "It's unavoidable," he suggested, with a glance around the room. "We must telephone the police." He turned back to Toby. "Why am I arguing with you?"

"I don't know, man." Toby's eyes were closed, but a smile flickered over his lips. "You can't argue with a dead man."

Banerjhee felt as if he might faint.

"Those fuckers," Toby opened his eyes, "weren't the fuckers we expected." He coughed bloody spittle from the corners of his mouth. "Wrong fuckers."

Banerjhee shook his head helplessly. "There are right ones?"

"Fucking Colombians," came the answer. "Which reminds me, don't worry, be assured, our Colombians will soon be here. They must have stopped somewhere for ammo and stimulants."

"But . . . so who. . . ?"

"Probably somebody who thought they had easy pickings here, clip us for stash or cash or both." He fought for air. "It won't make any difference, once I get to Hell. It better not, anyway."

Oh no, Banerjhee stopped himself from contradicting

tenderly, you're going straight to Heaven, Toby. There to join Esme in Eternity. He squeezed Toby's hand gently.

Toby made a very strange sound, a cross between a groan and a cry of exasperation, and said with obvious effort, "Hey."

"Yes?"

"You know the first thing they make you do in Purgatory?"

"No, Toby, I don't."

"They make you learn Windows 98." He inhaled sharply. "Top to bottom."

"What?" Banerjhee misunderstood. "Why?"

"Cause it's your ticket to Hell." Toby made wheezing noises which constituted, Banerjhee realized, Toby's new style of laughing.

Banerjhee suppressed a groan. "That's if you don't get reincarnated. That's if you don't go to heaven. That's. . . ."

"That's if there's anything at all," Toby said. "Fuck it. I had my fun." For some reason, Toby thought this summation both pitiful and funny. After his new form of laughter had subsided, he said to the ceiling, "Who shot the second .357 round?"

"You heard it?"

"Are you kidding?"

"I did."

"Huh?" For the first time Toby took his eyes off the ceiling and rolled them toward Banerjhee. "You did?"

"He was shooting Esme."

"You–?" Toby exhaled loudly and his eyes squeezed shut.

"He was shooting Esme," Banerjhee insisted.

"You. . . ." Toby disciplined his breathing to regular, short gasps. Finally he said, "It came back."

"The– Where?"

Toby's eyes flicked to his left and Banerjhee looked. On the floor about a foot to the left of the sliding glass door's casing gleamed the little steel frame and the pearl of a diminutive handle. The derringer lay upside down against

100

the baseboard, beneath a wall plug. It was probably the only place in the room that Toby had been able to see, once he'd fallen.

"Always shoot it indoors, BJ," Toby said to the ceiling. "That way you'll always find it."

Toby made the laughing sound. Banerjhee, who as of that moment had shot a gun exactly once in his life, and had no intention of shooting one again, saw nothing to laugh at.

Toby stopped laughing. "How did it go down?"

Banerjhee told him.

After a contemplative pause at the end of the story, Toby said, "I didn't see a third guy."

Banerjhee made no response.

"We could have taken two." Weaker yet, Toby added, "Esme was a great partner."

"How long were you two . . . partners?"

Toby narrowed his eyes. "Three, no, four years. Four years. She was the good cop." Toby smiled feebly. "But you probably figured that out already."

"I . . . beg your pardon?"

It seemed that Banerjhee's bewildered consternation might cause Toby to laugh himself to death. "Police officers!"

"I keep my badge up my ass," Toby gagged. "Right next to my brain. . . ."

"Police officers. . . ? But, but this isn't funny, Toby. What are you doing here? Right next door to me? To us? In the middle of nowhere? Nowhere. . . ." Banerjhee repeated stupidly. "Nowhere."

"Buying and selling our way up the food chain, of course. Trying to catch us some Colombians. We're good at it, too. We *were* . . . good at it." Toby's expression became serious. "Hey, BJ."

"Yes, Toby?" Banerjhee responded faintly, as if from one dream to another.

"They're still coming, you know. The Colombians. Wait. At some point, I will become speechless. Unable to talk. Shut up and listen. I'll blink my eyes. Uh, once for yes. Okay? Twice for no. Like on TV. You don't watch TV. Trust me. They do it all the time. It always works. BJ. Meanwhile, BJ, you need to get out of here. It's not their style to be late. It's not their style to cut people slack either, even when they're on time. Wait. . . ."

Toby's whispers had become nearly inaudible. "An ambulance might have been here by now," Banerjhee fretted aloud.

"Any normal paramedic would only fiddlefuck around long enough to insure that I really suffer before I check out. You ever watched them load somebody on a stretcher when they're scared? It's not pretty. Unless one of them's a vet, they will have no idea what to do with damage like this. There's nothing to be done anyway. I'm toast. I'm babbling," he forcefully added, obviously irritated. "Let's concentrate on you." Toby's chest heaved and his fingers convulsively grasped Banerjhee's with surprising strength. "BJ!"

"I'm here."

"Don't be here!"

Banerjhee cast an anxious glance at the rest of the room. "But if they weren't your Colombians, then who. . . ?"

"I have no idea. I'd like to know. Maybe I could trade the knowledge to the devil for ice water. Get your ass out of here."

Banerjhee only studied the room.

"All right," Toby rasped. "See what you can find on them."

"See what I. . . ?"

"You hanging around here just to watch me croak? Get out or go through their pockets!" Toby insisted with unexpected vehemence. "What's it going to be?"

For ten seconds Banerjhee sat on the floor next to Toby, holding the dying man's hand and blinking rapidly.

Then he crawled to the first corpse beyond the televisions, turned it over, and pulled off the ski mask.

He was much older than Banerjhee would have thought, fifty, maybe fifty-five. His hair was trimmed fairly short and completely white. The slug from the derringer had entered his throat at the larynx and nearly severed the man's spinal column. His head hung as if by a string and almost came off with the ski mask, which was about as unnerving as anything that Banerjhee had witnessed so far.

The dead man wore an unzipped flak jacket. Perhaps he had not been expecting as much trouble as he found. In the blood-soaked breast pocket of the denim shirt beneath it, Banerjhee found a slim wallet.

In the wallet he found a badge.

He sat back on his heels and looked at the second man, whom Esme had shot. Beyond, he could see the feet of the third man, whom Banerjhee had shot. Their flashlight shone straight up at the ceiling. Dust motes and smoke careened through its beam.

The badge was pinned to a leather flap. Under the flap was an identification card.

He scuttled over to Toby. "I think I wish these men had been your Colombians." He held the badge over Toby's face and angled it toward the televisions. "What does this mean?"

Toby squinted. A bright point of light, reflecting off the badge, danced over his face.

"I'll be a son of a fucking bitch," Toby said at last. "Does the face match the photo?"

"Yes."

Toby became visibly agitated. "Why didn't they fucking ID themselves? Why?" He spit blood on the badge. "Fucking dumb-ass Feds!"

Banerjhee narrowed his eyes at the badge as if it were too bright to contemplate directly. "Feds?" he asked stupidly.

"Can't you read? *United States Federal Marshal.*" Toby managed to spit blood at the wallet and Banerjhee winced. "See? Says right on the badge!"

Banerjhee held the badge to the light so he could read it. "So it does." He lowered the wallet and sat back on his heels. "So it does"

Toby's face, deadened no doubt of nearly all sensation, creased into a perfect mask of frustration subverted by amusement. "The goddamn Federal Communications Commission sent those guys in here. Fucking dumb-ass Feds. They were after Scramble Man. They thought me and Esme were Scramble Man!"

Banerjhee couldn't believe it. "Scramble Man? They sent three federal agents with machine guns to shut down a ten-watt television station?"

"Can't be too safe," Toby said bitterly. "Scramble Man. . . ." His laughter visibly sapped him. "This is fucked up. Esme and me thought you were Scramble Man. The FCC's surveillance was screwing up our drug sting so we were going to lend the feds a hand, you know? Dime you to them. Get you and them out of our way. Not only did it not turn out to be you, but those assholes thought he was us. Esme and me. Oh, hell, BJ," Toby rasped, "I've been a cop all my life. I was in the service, too. I have seen my share of fuckups. But this is one . . . fucking. . . ."

Toby's eyes turned from transparent glass to mirrors and back, which left Banerjhee with little doubt that he about to witness an important transition.

"No," Banerjhee said, after some thought. "They came here to rob you."

Toby gave that one some thought. "Okay," he said at length.

"Same difference. You and Esme and me have lit us up one federal marshal apiece."

Banerjhee had already done the math.

"Esme and me, we're well out of it. But BJ. You. . . . If the Colombians don't get you first. . . ."

"I'm never going to talk my way out of this," Banerjhee concluded dully. "Am I."

Toby made a tremendous effort. "They won't let you. Feds can't afford this shit. They will make you spend the rest of your life and all of your money defending yourself. They have to cover their ass. They'll make their fuckup your fuckup and they'll do everything they can do to make it stick. Listen to me."

Banerjhee merely stared at the carnage.

"BJ?"

"I'm listening," Banerjhee said quietly.

"Shit," Toby coughed, "it'll be a year before they let you see a lawyer. Two years. That's the way those fuckers work nowadays. They can do anything they want. They're fucked up. You can consider that an informed opinion. Listen to me. I'm a . . . I was a . . . a goddamn . . . a cop. . . ."

Along with the *p* in *cop* came the last of Toby's spittle, but he persisted in moving his lips at the ceiling by way of continuing to give Banerjhee advice. "You might as well have yourself a fling, BJ. I'm not kidding. Me and Esme have ruined your life. Do you understand this?"

"No," Banerjhee said simply. "But I take your point."

"Where's your old lady?"

"Madja?" Madja. He hadn't thought of Madja in. . . . One hour? Two? "Chicago," he said, as if he didn't quite believe it.

Toby brightened. "Can you get a hold of her? Without leaving a trail, I mean?"

Banerjhee considered this. "Possibly."

"Good. Tell her to hire a lawyer and sit tight. Maybe she'll be okay, maybe they won't be able to ruin her too. Tell her to find a guy with experience who hates the government. It's for her own good. Tell her. . . ." Toby stopped, His lips made little dry smacking movements, like a beached fish. "She's gotta write you off."

Banerjhee retrieved the glass of beer from the coffee table, dipped two fingertips into it, and touched them to Toby's lips. After three or four applications Toby could whisper audibly again. "Tell her we, I mean Esme and me, tell her we're real . . . sorry about this."

"This is not your fault," Banerjhee said. "It was a matter of chance. Simple chance. A coincidence. A mistake." He wondered whether he believed it.

"That reminds me. Take the money."

"Take the. . . . What money?"

"The lottery money. Take it, BJ."

Banerjhee looked at the coffee table. "But it's yours," he stammered before he realized what he was saying.

"Can't use it." Toby's amused features appeared to be clinging to his face, uncertain of their purpose. His lips no longer moved at all. "It's yours, now. I'm giving it to you. The lottery gave it to me; I give it to you. I won, now it's your turn, and if you don't get your ass in gear, some Colombian's going to win it. I can't think what's keeping them. Maybe they heard the shooting and took off. More likely they found some pussy with the ammo and stimulants. Normally the fuckers are extremely prompt. Get out, BJ. Have yourself a ball, man, before this shit catches up with you. Take the money, take anything you want. There's some blow in that drawer, there. . . ."

Banerjhee looked that way. "Blow?"

Toby blinked and said, "Cocaine."

Banerjhee frowned. "What would I want cocaine for?"

Toby blinked some more, then screwed up his features into a mask of pained concentration. "Everything here is confiscated," he rushed on, "from drug dealers or thieves. How about the Beamer? Take the Beamer. It was impounded from a chop shop. They did a great job. Key's on a hook in the kitchen. You'll love it, BJ; it's a rocket. Outrun the cops with it. Live a little. Make sure you go up in a ball of flame or you'll rot in maximum security for the rest of your life with nothing but a small black-and-white television and no habeas corpus."

"You expect me to just leave you to the Colombians?" Banerjhee protested.

"My train's in the station, BJ," Toby assured him. "Ain't nobody gonna do shit to me."

"Toby." Banerjhee dipped his fingertips in the beer and anxiously touched them to Toby's lips. But the tip of Toby's tongue had swollen behind his clenched teeth, and the lips no longer moved.

"Toby?" Banerjhee whispered, his own voice barely audible. "Toby, are you dead?"

Toby blinked once.

TEN

Here are some things Banerjhee Rolf considered, as he drove through the night.

An entity less than ten kilometers in diameter drives the entire Crab Nebula—which is as much as to say it makes it glow, so that we here on earth, some 6500 light-years away, can marvel at it.

The Crab Nebula is ten light-years across. Ten light-years, as most folks know, is how much distance a beam of light can cover in a straight line in ten years. A year in this context is the one we're all familiar with, the time it takes the Earth to make one revolution around its sun.

Light travels at 186,000 miles per second. Sixty seconds per minute times sixty minutes per hour times twenty-four hours per day times three hundred and sixty-five days per year times ten years. . . .

And here, while his mind did some arithmetic, Banerjhee watched his windshield movie for a while, which at night in central Nevada consists in the main of a lot of darkness, a few road signs, and very occasionally another pair of headlights. One must beware of deer and cows and horses and other large livestock, too.

The answer, his brain eventually announced, is about sixty trillion miles.

Let it be round like, say, the Earth. Sixty trillion miles is the diameter. The circumference of the Crab nebula would then be. . . .

The dash lights of the BMW were an eerie reddish-orange. Martian orange. The speedometer stops reporting at 240 kilometers per hour. On-board GPS readouts insure that the vehicle not be lost unless, as Banerjhee presumed, he were to venture into antipodal latitudes for a prolonged gaze at the Southern Cross.

. . .A little less than two hundred trillion miles. The circumference, that is. Set all aglow by an object six miles across. Interesting. Let's go backwards. Forwards or backwards, if this Beamer could approximate the speed of light, it would take it. . . .

The seats were black leather. An air-freshening piece of cardboard shaped like an evergreen tree hung from the rearview mirror. No accounting for taste, but its perfume failed to mask the rancid odor of scorched crack that permeated the car's interior. Crack cocaine, that is. Carbon 17, hydrogen 21, nitrogen oxide 4. Another one of those pesky alkaloids and not nearly so . . . interesting, yes, that's the word, not nearly so interesting as some of its cousins.

. . .At the speed of light it would take a little over thirty years to circumnavigate the entire nebula. Interesting coincidence, Captain Joshua Slocum took only a tenth that amount of time to circumnavigate the entire planet Earth, at a somewhat more leisurely pace, in his home-made gaff-rigged ketch, *Spray*. In Samoa, Fanny Stevenson made a gift to Slocum of the four volumes of Mediterranean sailing directions so cherished by her deceased husband, Robert Louis. Will there one day be such voyageurs to the Crab Nebula, and pertinent, multivolume sailing directions? No, Arthur C. Clarke famously replied to a similar question, any race of beings so advanced as to achieve interstellar travel will blow itself up first.

No matter. Tonight, with equal parts physics and imagination, the voyage is accomplished by the intergalactic Beamer pilot. Extraordinary. . . . In order to circumnavigate the Crab Nebula our light-speed pilot would have to first squander the sixty-five hundred years necessary to get from Earth to the Crab Nebula in the first place.

Once you hit the California border, well, you might as well keep on going. Time would stop for him aboard, of course, at that pace. So many books, Banerjhee used to say to himself, contemplating his library, so little time. Would the gainfully unemployed voyageur get around to reading all of Feynman's *Lectures?* Or Proust? Thackeray? Trollope? Will the devil's library contain something other than Windows 98 manuals?

He'd set about putting the $45,000 under the spare tire in the trunk. Not particularly ingenious, but he couldn't think where else to stash it. In the trunk he discovered, quite by accident, under the rug, a panel in the left-hand wheel well. An extra key on the Beamer key fob unlocked it. Inside he found a 9 mm automatic pistol, a shoulder holster with harness, a spare clip, a half-empty box of shells, and a rectangular patch of leather with a belt-loop on one side and Toby Pride's badge on the other. In a pocket under the badge was his police identification card, with photograph. His real name was Thomas Ford.

Banerjhee figured he'd stick with Toby, the name he knew. No sign of Esme's identification.

It made sense, Banerjhee mused, to have placed the secret compartment under the fender opposite the one with the gas filler cap. The neck connecting the cap to the tank would have taken up most of the available space under in the right fender well. Logical placement. Optimum embodiment. He recalled that the car had been confiscated from a drug dealer. So it all made sense.

Sort of.

In the hurtling dark he looked around and wondered what other secrets his vehicle might possess. Though the speed control kept the speedometer pegged at 84 miles per hour, he could hardly hear the engine. The tachometer read a mere 2750 revolutions per minute. The redline didn't begin to sweep the engine's upper range until 7600 rpm. If he knew the tire size and the differential ratio, he could calculate the Beamer's top speed, minus a little aerodynamic drag and tire friction, but, as almost anybody else in the world excepting himself might point out, why don't you just step on it, dude, and see what she'll do? You're in the middle of Nevada at midnight, for goodness sakes. You haven't seen another vehicle for an hour.

The nice thing about a sun roof is you can see the sky. Too bad this thing won't steer itself, Banerjhee thought, although, he supposed, that'll probably be the next step. Just tell the car where to go. The driver will watch the night sky while his vehicle proceeds safely toward his destination. That night, however, central Nevada was overcast. Too bad.

After bathing and changing his clothes he stopped by the garage for a last look at his library, with its floor to ceiling shelves on four walls. Row upon row of books crowded the room, insulating it in fact and conception from the outside world. There was a shelf of horticultural works over the double casement that opened onto the garden. A section two feet wide and eight feet high was devoted to the literature of astrophysics. A hot-rodded computer on his desk could run *Mathmatica* like blazes and output a pretty wire-frame torus or Limaçon of Pascal or an embedding diagram to its large

high-definition screen in a trice. Not very portable, but who's
going anywhere? Banerjhee was going somewhere. He didn't
have the time or possibly even the capability of deleting from
his computer any and all references to Sam in Chicago. After
a moment's thought he set an old DOS utility to a standard
called 'military wipe' and turned it loose on the hard drive.

Maybe he could at least take along Shapiro and Teukolsky's
hefty *Black Holes, White Dwarfs, and Neutron Stars?*
Unemployment had freed up countless pleasurable hours to
pour over the six hundred pages of this dense text. Its cover
depicted its own embedding diagram, in which a red line
traced the path of a compacting cosmic body, an asteroid or
planet or star or subatomic particle, as it spiraled through
the yellow grid of space-time toward the funnel-like warp of
infinite gravity. Space-time so radically distorted that, it is
postulated, if one were able to remain coherent in conscious-
ness and body under these extreme conditions, one would
be able to see the back of one's own head.

How's that for paranoia?

But he settled for Simon Mitton's little classic, *The Crab
Nebula.* Along with its many virtues, readability among them,
and although it lacks mathematics almost entirely, the Mitton
text has many illustrations. Among them are three photo-
graphs of American Indian petroglyphs depicting the appearance of what the contemporary Chinese astrologers called a
"guest star." Like the Chinese observations, the Native
American rock paintings date from the 11th century. Prime
among the latter, so far as Banerjhee was concerned, is the
one discovered in Chaco Canyon, in New Mexico, only in
1972. Just to give us descendants some perspective, its artist
depicted a human hand alongside a crescent moon and a
strange, ten-pointed star. Calculations tell us that a quarter
moon definitely occurred in conjunction with the supernova,
probably on July 5, 1054, which corroborates with the

precisely dated Chinese observations. The hard part to believe about the petroglyph is that the moon and its guest are about the same size as the hand. Banerjhee had often held his hand up to the sky, adjacent every phase of moon, and wondered. Try it for yourself. Be sure to hold your hand at arm's length. Does there live the star-gazer who does not lament the fact that no supernova has occurred in our own galaxy since the invention of the telescope?

But fugitives, as Banerjhee imagined, must have very little time to read. So he settled on a telescope, its tripod, a lined parka, and a pair of warm gloves. It would be cold in Nevada.

Sacramento had come and gone before he figured out how to operate the hands-free phone, the controls to which were built into the rim of the Beamer's steering wheel. Undoubtedly, calls on the Beamer's phone could be tracked. But it couldn't be helped. Heeding Toby's advice he didn't try to call Sam in Chicago. Instead he left a message on Madja's password-protected voicemail at her office extension, which she would check on Monday at the latest. Cautiously he mentioned neither Sam, nor Chicago, nor where he himself was calling from.

"Madja. This is your husband. I. . . ." A lump formed in his throat, and he nearly hung up in order to compose himself. Instead he blurted, "I love you. Save this message. It might well turn out to be the only record of this version of the following story. Listen carefully." Without emotion he sketched the evening's events. The tale required three additional calls to her extension, as its host computer yielded only five minutes of recording time per message. Toward the end of the last call he said, "I think Toby Pride's assessment of my situation quite accurate. I know this idea will offend your sense of fairness. On the other hand, we've had a wonderful life. Many people can't say as much. A protracted

114

stay or, god forbid, a lifetime, in a prison cell—no matter the duration—deprived of your company, my books, the garden . . . the balance of my life bodes a protracted sojourn of no quality, crude life-support, a stasis monitored and enforced by bureaucracy. You would not wish this purgatory on me. Few are the humans on whom we might invoke it at all."

Banerjhee blinked. "I'll have to call you back."

He terminated the connection.

For half an hour, he just drove. He passed through Aurora, a former gold and silver mining town at the edge of the foothills of the Sierra Nevada. At the western edge of town a larger-than-life bronze placer miner kneels over his pan, right beside the freeway. On the eastern edge the dial of a large clock surmounts the gates of the town cemetery. Strictly observing the speed limit, Banerjhee had a good look at these twin specters of fortune.

Once past Aurora, where the freeway begins to climb the gentle western slope toward Donner Pass, he dialed Madja's extension for the last time.

"So, my little bird, do not think me unsettled by my narrowed prospects. It's a beautiful night, and I'm of lucid perspective. Not a cloud in the sky. I'm climbing toward the stars. Months or years in a prison hold no appeal, no more than foreshortened health brought on by constant anxiety. I've already spent too many years beguiled by walls and security clearances and climate-controlled air and row after row of fluorescent lights, and we won't even speculate about the noise. Daytime soap operas? I don't think so. Chance or destiny brought me to you, and chance or destiny has separated us, as, sooner or later and in any case, it will and must. So now we know it's sooner. Most people don't get to realize that much. At least I get to say goodbye." He pensively added, "Who would ever have thought, though, that chance or destiny would have taken the form of me gunning down a federal marshal?" He laughed and sat up in the seat to bring his mouth closer to the microphone. "By mistake, if anybody's listening!" He slouched back into the form-fitting leather. "It was almost as if I'd been training for the moment my entire life."

The voice-mail computer interrupted with a tone to tell him he had thirty seconds to complete his message, then beeped. "I have thirty seconds. I probably won't call again, unless, unless I need to tell you I love you. Again. Because I do. And Sam. Sam too. Little else ever really mattered. Goodbye Madja."

He forced himself to depress the button on the rim of the steering wheel to terminate the connection. It felt as if some remote ancillary device, far removed from his soul, had performed the task.

"My little bird," he told the windshield.

An hour later he crested Donner Summit. Seventy-five hundred feet above the San Francisco Bay and three hours east of it, he'd intended to stop and set up the telescope, if only for half an hour. But by the time he got there the sun was almost up. His beloved celestial objects had receded beyond his reach, obscured by the light of dawn. Too bad. It was as much altitude as he'd managed in quite some time. What with Madja's job and his desire to keep a low economic profile, the priority of stargazing journeys to high places had slipped in status.

The road was clear, but a few inches of recent snow, clean and white, reflected the alpine glow, and deeper drifts lay scattered in the low places among the north-facing crags of bald granite and beneath clusters of dark conifers that loomed over the pass. He gave fifteen minutes to the scenic overlook on the east side, long enough for an introspective gaze down on Donner Lake. The fascination of what had happened there, in 1846, wants only an active imagination to rekindle. But all Banerjhee could think about was that last thirty seconds of voicemail.

He continued past Truckee to Verdi, pronounced by the locals as Vaird-eye, which he remembered as the first truck stop on the California-Nevada border. There, much to his surprise, he found a full-blown casino hotel, side by side with the fueling operation. How many years had it been since he'd passed this way? He couldn't say. He gassed the Beamer and took the precaution of parking it behind the hotel, where it couldn't be noticed from Interstate 80. He reserved a room. He had to use a credit card, which he knew would haunt him if he ran long enough, but what were the chances of that? And what was he supposed to do about it? Reinvent himself as an accomplished criminal?

Before going to his room he nursed a beer at one end of the casino bar, where he had a ringside overview of a roulette table. It didn't take long to realize he would require a bigger game, but he followed the play and soon felt comfortable with its simpler moves. At dusk he would push on to Reno. Once you hit the California border. . . .

It was two beers and almost an hour before he felt sufficiently unwound to take the elevator to his room and surrender to some much-needed sleep. But his dreams were many and complicated and sharded, interloped with thundering diesels and airhorns and the crash of two or three dozen cubes periodically dispensed into a plastic bucket by an ice machine, which was just across the hall from his room, in its own niche, with two dead video poker machines and a soft-drink dispenser.

Late that afternoon he scanned all the news programs on the hotel television. The ratio of pornography and music videos and sitcoms and old westerns to hard news programs was about the same as that of the diameter of the Crab Nebula to that of its pulsar, but what news he could find made no mention of the murder of five law enforcement officers in California, no Massacre at Walnut Creek. Maybe the scene had not been discovered? Unlikely. So maybe the authorities were keeping it a secret. Come on, he chided himself, sitting on the edge of the bed with a remote in his lap. At the very least the three feds were wired to some sort of home base. Yes? No? Isn't that the way they work? Officer down and all that?

Well no, he surmised. If they're moonlighting, probably not.

He recalled backing the Beamer into the street. It was just as well that Toby had loaned it to him because the dead feds had blocked his own driveway with a black Ford Excursion, which left the blue Peugeot inaccessible. He had paused at the foot of Pride's driveway long enough to stop worrying about how the Beamer knew it was dark enough to turn its lights on by itself, and to spend five minutes figuring out how to turn off the CD player which, after thinking about it while he was backing up, abruptly decided to blast him with music he didn't know enough to call gangsta rap. Toby must have kept the crack dealer's CD collection. That's deep camouflage, he thought, exhaustingly deep. He found in this a glimpse at how schizophrenic the lives of the two narcotics agents must have been. How far did one have to go to project the image of a drug-addled entrepreneur, while remaining the guy who would make the pinch? It seemed a gulf capable of devouring all the energy made available to it.

As he sat in the idling Beamer thinking such thoughts, a flat-black HumVee materialized in the dark street not seventy-five yards in front of him. He wouldn't have been more startled if it had been a Stealth bomber. Instinctively,

Banerjhee let his foot off the brake. The Beamer idled silently forward. He had to steer its right-hand wheels onto the shoulder in order to squeeze past the cable network's huge reconnaissance vehicle.

The machine crawled past, barely moving, and he was amazed by its size. Like the Beamer's its windows were blacked out. The Hummer was so high off the ground all he could see was a row of rivets along the bottom of the HumVee's side windows, just about level with the Beamer's roof. Once past it he saw in his side- and rear-view mirrors many sorts of antennae on the Hummer's roof, including a dish on a telescoping pole, retracted just then, encircled by a coil of thick cable.

Banerjhee fed the Beamer into the first available turn and headed for Nevada.

He had himself served a salad with a steak and three cups of coffee at the casino bar, whence again he followed the statistical inevitabilities of the roulette table.

In the parking lot he found lumps of dirty snow criss-crossed by multiple tire tracks. A cold front had brought with it a lowering sky, and the air had an Arctic tang to it.

He retrieved his parka. When he closed the trunk lid it wouldn't latch. He closed it again with a little more force. The third time the latch caught, but something fell from the car to the damp asphalt. He picked it up. It was a small disk about the size of a quarter and three-eighths of an inch thick, dangling a four-inch length of insulated wire with a dab of silicone caulk on one side, the better to adhere the device to the inside of the bumper, he thought, and which, almost without a doubt, the mountain cold had hardened sufficiently to cause the bond to fail. He had never seen one before, such a small radio transmitter, such a bug.

Banerjhee zipped up his parka and let the obvious thoughts

surf through his mind. Certainly a police force likes to keep track of its undercover employees. Or maybe the Colombians like to keep track of them? Or conceivably the bug was left over and forgotten from previous surveillance? Maybe Scramble Man had caught on to Toby and Esme and put it there to keep an eye on them. But that seemed remote. Aha. Haha. Hahaha.

Banerjhee took a turn around the casino parking lot. A hundred yards away, traffic of every description rolled down the grade into Nevada, or labored up it toward California. Cars, motor homes, and big rigs pulled into and out of the fueling station adjacent the casino, slush streaming off their tires. It was snowing in the granite escarpments above Verdi. If the storm were big enough, the authorities would close Interstate 80 between the exits closest to the snowline on either side of the mountains.

He fingered the transmitter like a string of worry beads. He could easily disable it, he supposed. But what good would that do? It would indicate to whoever was tracking the car that the bug had been discovered. He wondered about the range of the thing.

Alternatively he could stash it under the bumper of any westward-traveling vehicle. Maybe better, another eastbound one. But he didn't like that idea. He'd already been involved in a case of mistaken identity. Once was enough.

On his second pass around the casino he dropped the bug into the middle dumpster, in a row of three, because it was full. Maybe a truck would pick it up tomorrow and take it to Idaho.

Tonight, meanwhile, just to play it safe, Banerjhee would skip Reno and push on south.

Once you hit the California border, you might as well keep on going. . . .

ELEVEN

He parked the Beamer on an innocuous back street and walked to the Strip.

The lights were big and omnipresent, and the last thing a body might consider attempting here was a browse among the stars of the night sky. Ambient light was prohibitive. If you want to see the night sky in Nevada, Las Vegas is the last place to try.

Banerjhee was not the first person to wonder where all that energy comes from. But there was so much of it that his sense of direction faltered. He wanted to do this right, but since he knew absolutely nothing about Las Vegas, he fretted that some unforeseen factor might get in the way; a worry informed, after all, by recent precedent.

So he walked around for a while. His slightly portly figure, much diminished by those of many of the people around him, fit right in. Enough of his fellow tourists, people of all colors and walks of life, looked confused and lost, too, so that Banerjhee had no trouble mingling. Many of them appeared to be on somnambulistic drugs. Of this horde the most obvious mechanically pulled the cranks on slot machines over and over and over, churning, as well, through drinks, cigarettes, and trays of silver dollars.

An interesting thing Banerjhee noticed about the slot players was that they could drink all they wanted, and smoke all they wanted, and eat all they wanted, because no matter what they did to body or mind, their gambling fortunes were pre-determined by a scheme built into a machine. This scheme is simple: The house takes almost all the money. Whoever is sitting at the machine at a certain statistically rare moment will see a certain return, let's say 1/X. Okay, let's say 2/X. Why not? X is a really big number.

The scope of the operation amazed Banerjhee. To put it simply, there are a lot of slot machines in Las Vegas.

The arm-crankers style themselves as players, too, which belies entirely the nature of their interaction with their game of choice, which is, except for cranking the arm, no inter-action. Soon enough Banerjhee found himself musing on the potential of a kind of inverted slot-player Turing Question: If the slot machine were a person, would it be able to detect that its player is not a computer?

All the way from Fallon to Las Vegas, well over 200 miles, it had been too overcast to set up his telescope. This was a bit frustrating to Banerjhee, though he was philosophical about it. After all, he might have come to Nevada at any time over the last twenty years for a look through a telescope. What with one thing and another, he hadn't.

He recalled the homily that life is something that happens to you while you're making other plans. Was that equally true, then, for death as well? Hmm. Had Feynman said that? He doubted it. It didn't feel funny enough for Feynman. Banerjhee also doubted that that's what had happened to him, precisely. He had married the woman he loved. By and by they had a son. By and by the son grew up, and grew up well. All of that had been planned, more or less. By and by there came the heart murmur. By and by Banerjhee's career had crashed or, more accurately, had been crashed. By and by, it got to be tonight.

Not planned. Not planned at all.

He narrowed the possibilities down to a place called The Crown, a "sawdust joint," so called, that was not on the Strip. But it seemed a big and sufficient operation. It had only one street door and no windows of course, a couple of restaurants and three bars but no dinner theater with comedy or live music. The Crown Casino was about gambling, with multiple television monitors for Keno and sports betting, and several each of poker, blackjack, craps and roulette tables. Three or four high-rollers were throwing money at one of the wheels, and smaller fish mingled among them. There was a fair crowd around that particular table, big enough to stay anonymous in, but not so big as to attract attention.

Banerjhee took a seat on a nearby barstool. The bartender was an older woman with hennaed hair, dressed in black slacks, white blouse and black vest with a pair of conchos on each hip. A little plaque pinned over her breast pocket said her name was Karen. Karen was very busy and clearly tired. The job was wearing her out. After a while, as she loaded glasses into an under-counter dishwasher, she paused for his order. Banerjhee asked for Ranier. Karen made a face.

"We carry 85 beers in here, mister, but Ranier isn't one of them."

"Never mind, the request was sentimental. Gosh," Banerjhee smiled and looked around. "You'd never know that once upon a time Ranier was probably the only beer you could buy in a place like this."

Karen looked up from her dishes and a wisp of hair fell over her face. She brushed it away and smiled. "Nah. We sold Hamm's and Olympia, then, too."

Banerjhee settled for a half-pint draft of a Pilsner he'd never heard of. "Not bad," he admitted, after a taste.

"Stick around. Come Christmas we get one from San Francisco that tastes like eggnog."

Banerjhee had already tasted that one. "No thanks."

"I hear that."

There were six people serious about the roulette game nearest him. Half again that many watched it.

Directly across the table a big man in a black western-cut suit, with glittering threads running through it to match his brand-new ten-gallon hat, watched a carefully made-up young brunette in a little black dress fritter away twenty dollars a bet, subtracted from his own rack of chips.

At one end of the table two mid-western looking women—tanless and overweight in roomy blouses and Bermuda shorts, with paste jewelry, and horn-rimmed glasses with mildly tinted lenses and rhinestone initials in the blind spot of the right lens, their tinted hair in bouffants, one reddish brown and the other reddish black—bet some kind of system. They skipped every other drop of the ball in order to consult with each other.

In between these two couples sat a pair of college kids. He was slim in khakis and oversize tee-shirt with a backwards baseball cap. She wore a plain, short black skirt that showed off her tanned legs, with a halter top under a jacket. They placed small bets and, win or lose, smiled sleepily; idling away the boy's refractory period, no doubt.

Banerjhee was just beginning to think the game too tame when a bearded old man elbowed his way to the rail between the two women and the collegials. This gaunt individual appeared to be well into his seventies and hale as they come. He wore canvas pants with padded knees, of a type favored by artichoke pickers, the cuffs tucked into knee-high, walking-heel boots so knackered that much of their leather no longer held any dye. Even though it was 65 degrees out on the street, he wore a heavy if threadbare long-sleeved blue and white

124

striped brakeman's shirt over long-johns and under a brown, much-worn leather vest topped off by a brown, sweat-stained felt hat. The whole ensemble was sufficiently battered to match the boots. From the breast pocket of the vest dangled the strings and medallion of a tobacco sack, at his hip he wore a clasp-knife holster on a thick black belt so worn it was molded to his hips, and the pants were additionally supported by a pair of woven horsehair suspenders. This old-timer stacked five chips on the felt and growled to nobody in particular, "Five hundred on th' twenty-two, for no other good goddamn excuse than I gotta start loosin' someplace."

The college girl didn't quite turn all the way around to look at him, but she wrinkled her nose and frowned at the boyfriend. The boyfriend traded places with her, the better to steal curious glances at the old man.

"Goddamn it, Jasper," the croupier said. "The last time you were in here, you spilled buttermilk all over my table."

"I ain't yet drinkin' no buttermilk, Chet," Jasper pointed out, rattling a rocks glass with ice and brown liquor in it. He drained half of it before adding, "But I will if somebody fetches me some. In the meantime, play ball."

"Just you behave, then," the croupier cautioned him. "Or we'll be receiving a visit from upstairs." He cast an eye aloft, and, while the old-timer gave this not a thought, Banerjhee did. Affixed to the ceiling above the table was a tinted hemisphere about eighteen inches across. Inside it would be a remote-controlled camera by means of which the management could keep an eye out for card counters and dice palmers and such.

The croupier called for last bets and dropped the ball.

"Sixteen," he crooned after a few seconds. "Sixteen, red and even." Not a murmur passed through the crowd as he raked in every chip on the table.

"Bourbon an' ditch," Jasper said to a cocktail waitress who

125

had appeared at his side. "Got any a them jalapenos?" He pronounced it without a tilde.

The ladies from Indiana and the college couple gave Jasper some elbow room. A thousand dollars had been wagered and lost, but nobody quit the game.

"Why here's old Jasper," said the bartender. Banerjhee turned to find her leaning against the back bar with her feet up on the rim of the undercounter sink, massaging her calves with a pained look. "My dogs are barking," she affably admitted. She pointed with her chin. "Jasper's one of your original, independent prospectors. You don't see his kind in Vegas so much any more. The town's gotten more. . . ." she waggled the flat of a hand parallel to the floor, "family oriented. Especially out on the Strip."

"He certainly appears to be colorful," Banerjhee said.

The waitress grunted. "Stick around. Cheap booze and camp-fire cooking have eaten a hole in his gut. He'll be swaddling that bourbon in buttermilk in a round or two. See over there?" She pointed across the casino. At the street door the waitress who had taken Jasper's order handed some cash to a young man dressed like a bellhop, who turned and left. "He's going for jalapenos and buttermilk." Karen pronounced it without the tilde, too.

"Jasper must be a good customer."

"You know, he's not as much trouble as he looks. But some people, especially ones from out east, he makes them nervous."

"Is he really a prospector?"

The bartender nodded emphatically. "Oh, yes. Got a jackass and everything. He spends eight or nine months a year in the mountains north of Tonopah, living out in the open. Nobody knows where, exactly. Jasper's got his secrets. Two or three times a year he turns up with a poke full of nuggets, some of them quite large, they say. He brings them down here because there's a jeweler in town he trusts. The jeweler assays the gold and pays him in cash."

"Sounds like frontier days."

"The real deal," she agreed. "After he visits the jeweler, Jasper always comes here."

"Why here?"

"Mr. Crown, the guy who started the place? He and Jasper were in the same outfit in the war."

"Which war?"

"Korea."

"Of course. Is the owner still as spry as Jasper?"

Karen set her feet back down on the duckboards and stood up to draw herself a glass of soda water. "Nah." She fingered a pill out of the side pocket of her vest, chased it down with the water, and shook her head. "He died upstairs in the arms of a hooker about five years ago. Biggest funeral we had in Vegas since Liberace died. His son runs the operation now. Runs it good, too. Kept on all us old-timers. Didn't turn the cafe into a day-care center. Like that."

"The son's okay with Jasper?"

"Sure," she shrugged. "Tommy Junior grew up knowing him. As far as he's concerned, Jasper lends an air of authenticity to the place. Hell, you go out on the Strip? There's places that hire guys to come in and act like Jasper, if it's the fashion."

"I believe it."

"Let's see if you believe the next part."

I'm fresh out of incredulity, Banerjhee thought. "Try me," he said aloud.

"Okay." Karen lowered her voice. "Soon as he gets paid off, Jasper makes a straight head for the Crown. Right away he starts drinking and getting a heat on and losing money. This behavior of course attracts a certain predatory animal.

At some point he'll pick out a girl and take her up to his room."

"Really?" Banerjhee said.

"I know," the bartender assured him; "I don't like to think about it either. But you know what the deal is?"

"Do I need to?"

She lowered her voice even further. "He makes them give him a bath."

When it was clear she'd stopped, Banerjhee said, "That's it?"

"So help me." She raised a hand. "It's God's truth." She touched his sleeve. "In two shakes the girl's paid off and Jasper's back on a table—barbered up, thirsty, and throwing his money away. And you know what else?"

"No. What else?"

"He'll carry on till he loses every goddamn dollar."

"All that hard-earned money?"

"Every cent. Many's the time Tommy Junior has to front him gas money to get him back to his claim." She shook her head. "Every cent. I've watched it thirty or forty times, ever since I came to work here." She added, enunciating carefully and clearly, "Which was quite some time ago."

Banerjhee eyed Jasper with renewed interest.

"I asked him about it once," Karen volunteered.

"What did he say?" Banerjhee asked, not turning around.

"He told me he likes being broke. How's that for a philosophy?"

Banerjhee pursed his lips.

"Here come the groceries," Karen observed. Banerjhee looked across the room in time to see the bellhop returning from the store. He bore a plastic sack in each hand and headed straight for the bar, but it was the party that followed him through the street door that caught Banerjhee's eye. This consisted of three men, each dressed more or less alike. Each affected a bushy moustache, each could have used a haircut, each wore an oversized flannel shirt with its tail outside his jeans, each wore thick-soled walking shoes, and none of them manifested the dazed concentration affected by most people who are just setting foot into the casino of their choice.

The trio made an unhurried survey of the room, as if they had divided the chore evenly among themselves.

Banerjhee turned his back on them. "I think I'll have another glass of beer."

The bartender said, "You going to finish the one you got?"

"Well," Banerjhee said, "I prefer my beer very cold."

Karen shrugged and retrieved a frosted glass from the under-counter refrigerator.

Beyond her, in the back-bar mirror, two of the men were clearly reflected. After a moment the third reappeared and introduced the others to a large man in an impeccably tailored suit, but nobody shook hands. The security guard pressed one hand to the side of his face, the better to hear instructions from his ear-piece. He gestured to the three men, and they followed him through an unmarked door just beyond the teller's cage. The door, rippling in the mirror among the bottles, closed behind them.

"We have a winner," said the croupier. "Pay the line bet."

Banerjhee turned to find the two midwestern women twittering as the rake pushed six twenty-dollar chips at them. The man in the Stetson beamed approvingly. "Oh Daddy," his girlfriend said, "They won a hundred dollars."

"Well shit, honey," the man in the Stetson boomed, pointing his cigar, "you won, too."

"Oh?" She looked from the two ladies to the table.

"Pay even," said the croupier, doubling her twenty-dollar bet.

"I won!" she squealed.

"Where's my the goddamned buttermilk? Where's my jalapenos?" Jasper demanded. "Play ball, goddammit."

"Place your bets, please. . . ."

Banerjhee took a sip from his new beer, not stalling, exactly, but judging his chances. Should he change locations? He glanced around the casino. Perhaps not. He might not even get out the door. He eyed the players around the roulette table. He liked the idea that the casino knew Jasper. He liked that the casino knew that if they left Jasper alone, he would lose all his money. He liked that, excepting the piddling wins from which hope springs, everybody around the table seemed to be losing reasonable amounts of money.

Jasper finished his bourbon and water and stood with his modest belly against the table rail, flaking a stack of chips from one hand to the other. When everybody else had laid their bets, Jasper abruptly arranged eight one-hundred-dollar chips along the edges of the square enclosing the unbet 24, with a ninth chip in the middle. "Play ball, goddammit."

"No more bets," said the croupier. "No more bets."

Everybody lost.

"Buttermilk!" growled Jasper, holding up his empty glass.

One of the ladies from Indiana retrieved a purse from the shelf beneath the table and balanced it on the rail while her partner scooped out four double fistfuls of twenty-dollar chips.

A clean-shaven young man dressed just like a cowboy appeared and stacked a modest row of chips in front of the next-to-last spot of elbow room at the table, right between Banerjhee and the front door.

Banerjhee beckoned to Karen.

"Can I get some chips?"

The bartender looked at him for a moment but didn't say anything. Her glance conveyed that she hadn't figured him for a gambler, that it occurred to her to warn him off it, that instead she would do her job, which was to push a button on the house phone behind the bar.

Almost immediately a cashier appeared. She was a pretty young woman in a short skirt with a bustier whose stitching formed a crown beneath her bare shoulder blades, and she wore her exchange desk much as a cigarette girl would wear her box of wares, on a strap around her neck. She looked at Karen, and Karen nodded at Banerjhee.

"Yes, Sir," the cashier smiled pleasantly. "Cash or credit?"

"Cash," Banerjhee said.

"And the amount?"

"Forty-five thousand dollars."

TWELVE

"We'll have to go to the cage for that amount, sir."

"The cage?" Banerjhee hesitated. He liked things as they were. He had the bar at his back; he could play the table while facing the front door; he was on speaking terms with the bartender. The cage seemed far away.

"Sir?" The cashier glanced over her shoulder.

In for a penny, in for a pound. Ain't no hill for a high-stepper. Once you hit the California border, you might as well keep on going.

"Coming. Yes. . . ."

He followed as she threaded a path through various bar patrons and migrating knots of people, down the middle of a double aisle of jangling, swooping, whirring, zooming slot machines sounding altogether like a herd of berserk calliopes.

The girl led him to the teller's cage hard by the door into which the three men in flannel shirts had followed the security guard, and said, "Have a nice evening, sir."

He thanked her.

The man in the cage said, "May I help you?"

From the inside pocket of his lined windbreaker Banerjhee produced Toby Pride's lottery prize, one-hundred-dollar bills in four packages of one hundred bills each, and one bundle of fifty hundred-dollar bills bound by a rubber band.

The parka was navy blue with a reflective yellow stripe around the underside of its collar. He touched its fabric as if it were an unfamiliar textile. Normally he would wear the jacket to ward off cold and moisture during nocturnal stargazing. But he'd also chosen it for its large inside pocket, which was zippered.

The clerk thumbed the packets with an impressive nonchalance, as if ensuring to himself that each were a book in whose pages he had not misplaced a . . . a lottery ticket, maybe?

When he'd finished counting and stacking the cash the clerk made a note in a journal, parked the pencil behind his ear, and typed some figures on a keyboard.

As Banerjhee and the clerk waited for a response from the computer, the door to the right of the cage clicked opened. Banerjhee could not suppress a corresponding tic in his cheek just below the right eye.

The security guard who earlier had shown the three be-flanneled men through the door now stepped back through it. Without a sign that Banerjhee meant anything more or less to him than any other well-behaved customer, the man closed the door behind him, stood before it at parade rest, clasped his hands in front of him, and let his eyes drift around the room.

"Sir?" the clerk was saying.

"Oh, pardon," Banerjhee responded. "You asked me. . . ?"

"I asked whether you'd prefer any particular denomination," the clerk repeated patiently.

Behind Banerjhee a woman whom he hadn't noticed cleared her throat. Behind her a man glowered over her shoulder.

Banerjhee hardly knew what to reply. Were they the same

denominations as cash? He had an efficiency factor to contend with. "Do you have a thousand-dollar chip?"

The clerk produced a small black lacquered tray embossed in gold with the golden Crown Casino logo. He placed a single blue chip on it, also embossed with a golden crown, and folded his hands.

"Yes," Banerjhee assured him, as well as himself. "That will do nicely."

The clerk stacked four chips onto the one already on the tray, quickly measured eight additional stacks against it, and showed them to Banerjhee.

"Excellent," Banerjhee said.

"Enjoy your evening, sir." The clerk pushed the tray beneath the barred window. "Next, please."

Banerjhee took away from the cage his tray of plastic disks and the definite impression that the sooner and more efficiently a gambler made his way through the house, the better the house would like it.

It would suit him, too.

He quickly threaded his way back through the tables and people and gaming machines to his favored roulette table where, to his comfort, the scene hadn't changed. The bartender acknowledged his return with a slight inclination of her head toward his beer, which stood on the bar with a coaster over it.

"Thank you," Banerjhee said. "I'd like a fresh one."

Without a word the bartender retrieved a frosty glass from the refrigerator. While she drew him a fresh Pilsner, Banerjhee laid his last twenty on the bar. "That's on the house," Karen said, "since you're playing."

"It's for you," Banerjhee told her.

"Thanks," she said simply.

"You're welcome," he said. "I've enjoyed talking with you." And he turned his attention to the game.

"No more bets, please," the croupier said, having loosed the ball. "No more bets." The ball made another turn around the polished outer groove of the wheel before it began to skip along the edges of the numbered cavities of the wheel's inner circumference, into one of which it dropped for keeps.

"Four," droned the croupier. "Four, even, and black. Pay the first dozen."

The number four had no chips on it, the midwesterners had covered Odd, and nobody had played the first dozen. Nobody said a word as the rake accrued to its master some fifteen hundred dollars idling about the table.

"Place your bets, please," the croupier said. Chips began to appear here and there on the felt. Nobody spoke. Banerjhee set two chips on double zero.

Jasper raised a bushy gray eyebrow and growled happily. "That juices her up." The two ladies next to him commenced a whispered conference. The sugardaddy, who had both hands in the front pockets of his trousers and a fresh cigar clenched between his teeth, alerted his lithe companion by clearing his throat. When she glanced over her shoulder, his chin pointed his cigar at Banerjhee. Banerjhee's mind was elsewhere. The girl's practiced appraisal took in his appearance, his tray of thousand-dollar chips, his two blue chips on double zero, and she proceeded to sister that bet with a hundred of her mentor's dollars. Then she smiled at Banerjhee, as if shyly. Banerjhee paid her no mind.

Jasper chuckled.

The midwesterners distributed twenty-dollar chips over the felt.

The cowboy put a five-dollar chip on 32, and another on Even.

Chewing a jalapeno, with a half-glass of bourbon and buttermilk on the rocks in one hand and four or five chips in the other, Jasper waited until all bets were down, then distributed two thousand dollars among various clean numbers, and Odd at the last moment.

"No more bets, please." The croupier dropped the ball. "No more bets."

Thirty seconds later, Banerjhee's two thousand dollars was gone. Only the cowboy won, doubling his five dollars on Even.

"Hot-diggety," the cowboy said, and snapped his fingers. He had a surprisingly high-pitched voice.

And so it went. Fifteen minutes later, simply by continuing to bet on double zero, Banerjhee had lost about a third of Toby Pride's lottery money. By the time he increased his bet to five thousand dollars a throw, a small crowd had gathered. The lithe brunette had long since bit her lip and reverted to laying twenty dollars on Even on one turn and Odd the next. One end of her backer's cigar had gone out, and the other end was chewed to pulp. The cowboy, having lost back his five dollars, throttled back to one- and two-dollar bets. The two ladies from Iowa were holding their own. Jasper had won fifteen hundred dollars and was hugely enjoying himself.

Banerjhee had ordered another cold beer to replace his warm one, and was just taking his first sip when a momentary alteration of pressure passed through the casino, as if the air conditioning had kicked off and back on. It should have been an unnoticeable, almost undetectable detail. But Banerjhee discerned it; Banerjhee, who was noticing details as he hadn't noticed them since a summer he'd spent in Switzerland.

Across the casino the unmarked door next to the cashier's cage was just closing, and three men in flannel shirts stood in front of it. One of them was talking to the security guard still posted there. The other two were looking straight at Banerjhee.

"No more bets, please," the croupier instructed his players. "No more bets."

137

Quickly Banerjhee took up a quantity of his chips and heaped them on double zero without counting them. An audible gasp escaped the little crowd.

"I'm sorry, sir," the croupier said, pushing the chips back at Banerjhee with his stick.

"Ah, shit, Chet," Jasper chided the croupier. "You gonna make him wait to lose?"

"Fourteen," Chet replied. "Pay fourteen, red, and even, pay the second dozen."

Banerjhee stood with his jaw set, watching the rake do its work. The cowboy won four dollars. The girls from Iowa came back even. Jasper lost a great deal of money, laughed, and tossed the croupier a hundred-dollar chip for a tip. The brunette lost twenty dollars, too, and had yet to tip anybody.

The croupier retrieved the ball and stood his rake upright on the rail in front of him. "Bets, please. Bets. . . ."

Banerjhee blinked and pushed the rejected chips right back onto the double zero. Eleven thousand dollars. Eleven chips were all he could hold in one hand.

"Whoa," said somebody behind the man in the Stetson, and a buzz disseminated through the outer crowd. Banerjhee's fellow gamblers, however, stoically placed chips around the table, superstitiously leaving, Banerjhee noted, three rows of breathing space between their bets and the green double zeros.

Gambling, Banerjhee thought with a wry smile, this is not.

"No more bets," the croupier announced. "No more bets."

As the ball fell Banerjhee stole a glance at the room. The crowd surrounding the table had increased, and individuals had begun to encroach upon the polite distance normally allowed a table's players. Banerjhee caught a brief glimpse of a flannel shirt, two or three shirts behind Jasper.

"Winner? W-winner!" exclaimed the croupier, his insouciance compromised by the unexpected.

138

"Son of a bitch!" Jasper yelled, sloshing a little buttermilk on the college boy next to him, who, himself astonished, paid it no mind. Exclamations erupted from the crowd. Banerjhee blinked.

He looked at the wheel.

He blinked twice.

The ball rode the double zero like a pearl on a merry-go-round.

"We have a winner," the croupier repeated, as if himself still uncertain of his pronouncement, but he was repeating himself to Banerjhee. Banerjhee looked up, looked around, looked back at the wheel. The ball still rode double zero. Across the table, nobody had understood the uncertainty in his eyes.

"We'll have to stop the game, sir," the croupier told him. Chet looked to the other players. "We'll have to stop the game." He turned to Banerjhee. "I hope you have a social security number."

Double zero had hit with eleven thousand dollars on it. "What are the odds?" Banerjhee asked dully.

"Thirty-six to one, ya fuckin'. . . ." Jasper laughed. "Ya fuckin' winner!" he shouted, and the crowd roared its approval. "Get him a calculator!" "No, a wheelbarrow!" "We'll help you count it!" "Eleanor, my camera!"

Each time Banerjhee's mind carried a number, from one column to another, he blinked. It had been like that all his life. "Three hundred and ninety-six thousand dollars," Banerjhee said to nobody in particular. "And no cents."

And no sense.

Aha. Haha. Hahaha. . . .

The crowd had increased by a similar multiple. People stood in ranks, shoving and standing tiptoe to get a look. Ten feet behind the big man in the Stetson, a woman was hoisted onto someone's shoulders.

A pit boss appeared on the other side of the croupier. Or perhaps he had been there all along?

"I'll – I'll have to stop the game, Sir," the flustered croupier said for the third time, looking apologetically from Banerjhee to his superior and back.

"Eh, Tommy Junior," said Jasper, closing one eye and waving his glass at the pit boos. "You come to witness yer shit blowed all to hell?" He laughed and gestured with the glass toward Banerjhee. "This ol' boy's fixin' to own you."

Across the table, between Jasper and the college kids, a man wearing a moustache and a flannel shirt appeared in the front ranks of the crowd. His eyes surveyed the scene and then, as they settled on Banerjhee, the fingers of his left hand unbuttoned his flannel shirt.

Banerjhee took up his tray, tipped its contents over the eleven chips on double zero, and showed the empty tray to the crowd. The noise crescendoed toward chaos and abruptly plummeted into breathless silence, so that everybody heard Banerjhee quietly say, "Let it ride."

The mob lost all restraint. Women screamed. Eyes bugged in the visages of responsible family men. Call girls checked their makeup. The chest thumped in the shirt of every true gambler in the room. Bouncers and security personnel radioed for instructions and got none back. A man inserted himself between the flannel shirt and the table and took a picture.

"Don't fuck with his luck!" "Get outta there!" "Quiet!"

Chet, the croupier, looked up from the heap of thousand-dollar chips and directly into Banerjhee's eyes.

The mob hushed.

"Let it ride, please," Banerjhee repeated.

The croupier turned to his boss. "The gentleman says he wants to let it ride, Mr. Crown."

Tommy Junior could not corral the expressions that overran his face. They metamorphosed it like time-lapsed film of a saprophytic fungus. In an instant his features bloomed through shock and surprise to defiance and satori and, in the next instant, decrescendoed through certainty, scorn, gloat, and triumph, before reassembling into their customary impassivity. Tommy Junior would not be consulting the actuarial tables on this one.

"Then the house will let it ride," Tommy Junior announced. "Bring the man a drink."

"No!" The crowd surged forward as a solid mass of humanity. Jasper and all of the original players clung to the brink of the table as they would to a taffrail in a hurricane. "Fool!" "Stop him!" "Don't let him do it!" Only Banerjhee and the croupier were accorded elbow room, as if in reverence.

Abruptly, the crowd shut up.

The thunderstruck croupier turned from his boss and slightly inclined his head toward Banerjhee. "Ride it is, Sir."

Banerjhee retrieved a blue thousand-dollar chip from the heap on double zero and handed it to Chet. "Thank you."

The din resumed. People in the front of the crowd explained to those behind them what was going on without taking their eyes from the table, while jostling to maintain their vantage against the pressures which threatened to overwhelm them from behind. Magnesium bulbs flashed continuously. Banerjhee now felt hopeful that events had assumed a critical momentum. The flannel shirt behind Jasper struggled to maintain its position in the second tier of the crowd, reappearing as if lifted by the crest of a wave only to disappear into the trough behind it.

The croupier nodded woodenly toward Banerjhee as if shocked into courtesy. Then he fingered the gratuity into his vest pocket and stood his stick upright on the rail. The crowd noise condensed into a kind of tumultuous hush. Seeing Chet's hands tremble, Tommy Junior allowed his eyes to emit a photon of disdain. "Bets, please," the croupier intoned. His voice cracked but he repeated the call, reattaining the firm and steady drone of his practice. "Place your bets, ladies and gentlemen. Place your bets."

Nobody placed a bet.

Down the bar to his right, where the crowd was hopelessly dense, Banerjhee sensed movement.

The croupier set the wheel to turning and loosed the ball against its rotation.

"Last call for bets."

Nobody laid down a chip.

"Bets. . . ."

Across the table Jasper glanced to his left, toward whispering at the far end of the bar, and he glanced to his right, toward Tommy Junior. Then he looked at Banerjhee.

The ball clicked against the berm of the groove and fell in. "No more bets, please." The sphere virtually twinkled. "No more bets. . . ."

Banerjhee no longer heard the clamor of bells, or outbursts from the crowd, nor the galloping circus music of a slot machine payoff, or the wrench of mechanical arms, nor camera shutters, or the voice calling a horse race or Keno digits. As if his mind had defaulted to some filtration software involving sound effects, only the ball remained audible. He had the feeling that, if he dared look around, he might discover that all motion, except that of the ball, had ceased.

But he didn't look around. He didn't want to make eye contact with a flannel shirt. Not yet anyway. But he needn't have worried. Every eye in the casino, even those that couldn't actually see it, even those which had other business to attend, every eye followed the ball in its course. Every eye, that is, except Banerjhee's, which had begun to perceive other things. The ball had yet to fall. Momentarily, Banerjhee couldn't even hear its careen. It was as if a tremendous pressure had popped his ears and left him deaf.

And then the ball skipped a numbered cell. The crowd gasped as if it had collectively forgotten to breathe. The ball tripped over the mouths of the numbered voids. Everybody watched. Chet and Tommy Junior watched. The flannel shirts watched. Now, of the entire crowd, only Jasper did not take his eyes off Banerjhee, and Banerjhee returned the stare. In the old man's eyes Banerjhee detected a vastness of desert and geology, of mountains and sunlight, of spangled, starry nights and frostbitten dawns and a composure derived of a lifetime passed inhabiting them. Banerjhee felt as if only Jasper, keenly observing, could really see him. The old man across the table moved his lips, but Banerjhee couldn't hear him. What could the old man possibly have said?

The ball had found its number.

Nobody spoke, The wheel turned in silence.

Somebody loosed a pair of dice, and they thumped over a table. Somebody pulled the handle of a slot machine. A third person opened a cellphone and said, "You're not going to believe this." Finally the croupier horsely croaked, "Twenty-five—" and cleared his throat. "Twenty-five," he repeated warmly, "Twenty-five, black, and even. Pay the third dozen. . . ."

Woodenly, as if traumatized, proceeding by rote through a motion he'd repeated sixty and seventy times an hour night after night for his entire career, Chet accrued with his rake twenty-three or twenty-four blue chips, the only chips on the table, gathered them in to himself on behalf of the house.

"Well, Toby Pride," Banerjhee said aloud. "There we have it."

"Easy come, easy go," Jasper said thoughtfully, to no one in particular.

143

A flannel shirt reappeared to Jasper's immediate right and elbowed itself some room at the table.

A house security guard whispered into Tommy Junior's ear, and Tommy Junior, raising an eyebrow, stepped back from the table, to reveal a second flannel shirt, which contrasted unfavorably with Tommy Junior's crisp pinstriped suit.

This second flannel shirt was also unbuttoned, and its owner's left arm lingered beneath it while the right arm brushed aside the security guard. "Rolf?"

The man in the flannel shirt had clear blue eyes and sandy hair and had not seen the sun in a long time.

"Banerjhee Rolf?"

"Yes," Banerjhee answered. "I am Banerjhee Rolf."

Across the table Jasper said, as mildly as if he were predicting rain, "That's the last time you're gonna push me, cocksucker," and cracked his rocks glass over the skull of some dude in a flannel shirt.

Buttermilk and bourbon, ice cubes and glass ticked over the felt of the roulette table. Little lines formed around the blue eyes facing Banerjhee, and their pupils flicked toward the ruckus.

The derringer was under Banerjhee's parka, nestled between his belt and the small of his back. Two spent cartridges remained, still and cold, in its two chambers.

Banerjhee reached for it anyway.